"Why would you ri~~sk your life to protect a~~ killer for me?"

"I know you don't want to hear this, but it's only fair I tell you. I'm crazy about you, Megan. I tried to deny it, tried to pretend the feelings weren't there, but they only grew stronger. Then last night when we kissed under the mistletoe, I had to face it. And unless I'm reading the signals wrong, you feel something for me."

She felt a lot more than something, but she'd been determined to blame it on her pregnancy-induced hormonal imbalance. "Has this ever happened before?" she asked.

"You're the very first. And for the record, it's against every rule in the book to get hooked on the woman you're required to protect."

Dear Reader,

This holiday season, deck the halls with some of the most exciting names in romantic suspense: Anne Stuart *and* Gayle Wilson. These two award-winning authors have returned together to Harlequin Intrigue to reprise their much loved miniseries—CATSPAW and MEN OF MYSTERY—in a special 2-in-1 collection. *Night and Day* is a guaranteed keeper and the best stocking stuffer around!

Find out what happens when a single-dad secret agent has to protect a beautiful scientist as our MONTANA CONFIDENTIAL series continues with *Licensed To Marry* by Charlotte Douglas.

The *stork* is coming down the chimney this year, as Joanna Wayne begins a brand-new series of books set in the sultry South. Look for *Another Woman's Baby* this month and more HIDDEN PASSIONS books to come in the near future.

Also available from Harlequin Intrigue is the second title in Susan Kearney's HIDE AND SEEK trilogy. The search goes on in *Hidden Hearts*.

Happy holidays from all of us at Harlequin Intrigue.

Sincerely,

Denise O'Sullivan
Associate Senior Editor
Harlequin Intrigue

P.S.—Next month you can find *another* special holiday title—*A Woman with a Mystery* by B.J. Daniels

ANOTHER WOMAN'S BABY

JOANNA WAYNE

HARLEQUIN®

TORONTO • NEW YORK • LONDON
AMSTERDAM • PARIS • SYDNEY • HAMBURG
STOCKHOLM • ATHENS • TOKYO • MILAN • MADRID
PRAGUE • WARSAW • BUDAPEST • AUCKLAND

ISBN 0-373-22639-X

ANOTHER WOMAN'S BABY

Copyright © 2001 by Jo Ann Vest

This edition published by arrangement with Harlequin Books S.A.

® and TM are trademarks of the publisher. Trademarks indicated with ® are registered in the United States Patent and Trademark Office, the Canadian Trade Marks Office and in other countries.

Visit us at www.eHarlequin.com

Printed in U.S.A.

ABOUT THE AUTHOR

Joanna Wayne lives with her husband just a few miles from steamy, exciting New Orleans. When not creating tales of spine-tingling suspense and heartwarming romance, she enjoys reading, golfing or playing with her grandchildren, and, of course, researching and plotting out her next novel.

Joanna loves to hear from readers. You can request a newsletter by writing her at P.O. Box 2851, Harvey, LA 70059-2851, or e-mail her at JoannaWayne@msn.com.

Books by Joanna Wayne

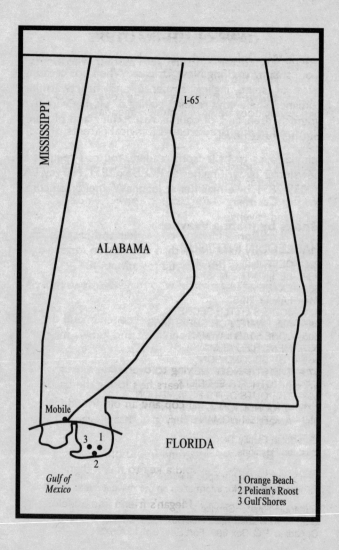

MISSISSIPPI

I-65

ALABAMA

Mobile

FLORIDA

Gulf of
Mexico

1 Orange Beach
2 Pelican's Roost
3 Gulf Shores

CAST OF CHARACTERS

Megan Lancaster—A surrogate mother who wants only to keep the unborn baby safe.

Bart Cromwell—A stranger in the town of Orange Beach, but does he have a hidden agenda?

Ben and Jackie Brewster—Biological parents of the baby.

Marilyn Lancaster—Megan's mother, a woman with secrets of her own.

Joshua Caraway—An escaped convict who's promised revenge.

John Hardison—Megan's co-worker and past lover, a man who may have more than one reason for seeing that Megan gives the baby up for adoption.

Mark Cox—A handyman who may have seen more than he's telling.

Fenelda Shelby—Megan's housekeeper. In and out of dozens of houses, she's seen a lot and knows more than she should.

Leroy Shelby—He's trying to overcome a drug problem, but his mother fears he's losing the battle.

Roger Collier—A local cop and an old friend from high school who seems very glad that Megan is back in town.

Sandra Birney—A longtime friend of Megan's mother, but does she hold a key to more than Pelican's Roost?

Penny Drummonds—Megan's friend and a lifelong resident of Orange Beach.

To everyone who loves to feel the warm sand between their toes, to build a sand castle at the water's edge or just to curl up with a good book with the rhythmic melody of the surf for background.
And to Wayne always.

Chapter One

December 4

Megan Lancaster turned onto the beach road the way she'd done hundreds of times before. Light gray clouds and patches of sunlight merged with the blue-green waters of the Gulf of Mexico. Swirling, heaving waves washed over white sand. Dozens of seagulls lined the bank. A light breeze danced through clusters of willowy sea oats.

Everything was the same as it had been so many times before when she'd escaped to the rambling beach house. Yet everything was different.

She shifted, trying to find a way to get comfortable behind the steering wheel of her new black sedan. It was useless, even though she'd splurged for the luxury model this time. Her bulging stomach prevented any kind of free movement and now she needed to go to the bathroom—again.

She pulled into a service station and reached for her brown loafers, which she'd shed after the last stop and thrown onto the passenger seat. There was no way she could bend far enough to reach her feet from behind the wheel, so she opened the car door and turned her body so that her legs hung out the open door. The shoes had fit perfectly when she'd shimmied behind the wheel four hours ago when she left her New Orleans town house, but now she had to struggle to force her feet into them. Swelling feet—another side effect of pregnancy that she'd been unprepared for.

Aching feet and cramped muscles notwithstanding, she waddled to the rest room inside the service station, took care of business, then purchased another bottle of springwater. She stretched the kinks from her neck and shoulders before getting back into the car and switching on the ignition.

One more stop before she could climb the steps at Pelican's Roost and collapse onto the inviting pillowed sofa. She hadn't been to the beach house in months and the cupboards would be as bare as Old Mother Hubbard's. And the only thing Megan did more often than go to the bathroom these days was eat. With that thought in mind, she reached her hand into the plastic bag on the passenger seat and pulled out a piece of dried fruit to munch on.

Twenty-three days until the baby was due. Twenty-three days with nothing to do but visit Dr. Brown, who'd already agreed to deliver the baby, and take life easy until she went into labor. With luck, she'd keep a low profile, avoid running into old friends with questions. Avoid having to explain the pregnancy when she wasn't married, and since her breakup with John over a year ago, wasn't even in an intimate relationship.

But she had her story ready, just in case. In fact she'd already shared it with Fenelda Shelby and Sandra Birney, the two women she couldn't possibly avoid. Both had bought her explanation, a mixture of half truths and basic omissions.

Fenelda had been the housekeeper at Pelican's Roost

for years, staying on to keep a watch over the house for Megan after her grandmother's death two years ago. Sandra Eloise Birney-Ramsey the third was her mother's best friend in Orange Beach and had been a jewel about watching over Megan's grandmother before her death. She'd never forgive Megan if she found out she was back at the beach house and didn't let her know. And nothing went on around Orange Beach that Sandra didn't find out about.

Driving slowly, Megan noticed another new high-rise condominium, one that had sprung up since her last visit, and a new restaurant as well. The growth in the area had been phenomenal over the last few years as more and more tourists discovered the emerald waters and sugar-white sands along Alabama's southern coast. The condos, restaurants and shops would all be packed once spring made it's grand appearance, but December was the off season. Before the snow birds arrived from the north to rent the condos for months at a time and after the summer tourists had returned to work and school.

Easing her foot onto the brake, she slowed and pulled into the parking lot of one of the new souvenir shops. She needed a pair of sandals to fit her swollen feet. The loafers were so tight that even shopping for basic supplies would seem like an endurance test.

She parked and pulled her cumbersome frame from beneath the wheel just as two lithe teenage girls exited the store, each with a large bag clasped in her hand. They moved so easily, almost as if they were floating on air, especially when compared to Megan's awkward stride.

All because of a baby who grew inside her. The now-familiar feeling washed over her, suffocating her, as if the gray clouds had fallen from the sky and landed on top of her. The feeling was incredible, unidentifiable. A feeling that everything was wrong in a world that up until a month ago had seemed totally right. But the despair never lasted long. A new and precious life was growing inside her.

She held on to the door of the car for support as the baby gave a few hard kicks before resettling in her womb. Then she put on what her grandmother used to call her "company face" and walked inside the store. With any luck at all, she'd get out without running into anyone she knew.

"Megan Lancaster, is that you?"

So much for luck. Penny Drummonds pranced toward her, makeup perfect, hair blond, short and bouncey, her size-six body fitted into a pair of designer jeans and a soft teal sweater. "It is you, and you're pregnant!"

"How'd you guess?"

"Oh, you," she said as they exchanged hugs. "You'll have to tell me everything. I didn't know you were even married. Last I heard, you were a dedicated career woman."

"I still am. How about you?"

"Same old stuff. Taking care of Tom and the kids. You'll have to come over for a visit. Is your husband with you?"

"Actually, I don't have a husband." It was almost worth the aggravation of running into Penny just to see the look on her face now. There was an awkward silence while Penny removed her foot from her mouth.

"But you're having a baby. That's wonderful."

"The baby's not mine."

Penny stared at her as if she wondered when Megan had escaped the loony bin.

"I'm a surrogate mother."

"I see."

Megan could tell from her expression that she didn't.

"Another woman's fertilized egg was implanted in my uterus."

Penny put a hand on Megan's shoulder, her facial expression telegraphing her doubt. "Even if it was yours, Megan, it wouldn't matter to me. Single women give birth all the time now. When's it due?"

"December twenty-seventh."

"A Christmas baby. You must be excited."

Not the word Megan would have picked, but she chose not to correct Penny. The bell over the door clanged, signaling that another customer had entered the store.

She and Penny both turned as a man in jeans and a gray sweatshirt stepped inside. He was nice-looking in a rugged sort of way—mid-thirties, light brown hair peeking from under a faded baseball cap, about six feet tall, lean and muscled.

Penny eyed him appreciatively but waited until he'd rounded a rack of T-shirts before commenting. "He'd make a nice Christmas present. Something to cuddle up with under the tree."

"Penny Drummonds, you have not changed a bit since high school."

"Sure I have. Now I only *look* and lust."

"I take it he's not a resident."

"I've never seen him around here before, and believe me, I would have noticed. He's probably married with six kids. If not, you should think about reeling him in while you're here on vacation."

Megan patted her protruding stomach. "I don't think I have the bait for that kind of catch."

"And speaking of catches, I'd better get home and cook for mine. Anyway, we'll have to get together for lunch one day. There's a new restaurant that makes a divine spinach salad with raspberry vinaigrette dressing. How long will you be in town?''

"A few weeks."

"Super. I'll call you."

Penny headed over to the clearance rack to check out the bargains and the sexy guy. By the time Megan made it back to the table of beach shoes, she could hear Penny's bubbling voice mingling with the man's much deeper one. Obviously she could flirt as well as look and lust.

Megan tried on several pairs of shoes, finally finding a set that didn't bind. She took the long way back to the checkout counter to keep from having to walk by Penny and risk having to answer more questions. It didn't work. Penny called to her from across the store. "Megan, you're not staying at your grandmother's big old house all by yourself, are you? It's so isolated and lonely on that part of the beach this time of year."

"It's home."

"You're much braver than me. I'd never stay by myself in that huge house."

No, but, thank you, Penny, for announcing all the details to the stranger who had quit rummaging through the clearance items to stare at her. Add uneasiness to the myriad emotions that played hopscotch with her hormones these days, hitting and missing in no particular order.

But unless the man was a serial killer or had some bizarre fetish for wobbling pregnant women, he wouldn't bother looking her up. Still, Penny had hit on a nerve. The last time she'd stayed in the beach house alone, when she was in the process of breaking up with John Hardison, she'd had trouble sleeping, had been wakened more than once by the creaking of the house and the whistling of the wind as it swept under the eaves.

All old houses have ghosts, her grandmother used to

say. *But only ghosts who harbor hidden secrets came back to haunt you. The rest of the ghosts just live within the happy memories held inside the walls of every home.* If that was true, the ghosts at her grandmother's house were probably sitting around thinking of her grandmother's keylime pie and the wonderful days of summer and sand castles, lemonade and running in the surf.

So why did she suddenly feel so alone and vulnerable at the prospect of staying at the house she'd always loved?

BART CROMWELL STOOD just inside the door of the souvenir shop and watched the pregnant woman climb into her car. She was extremely attractive, a classic beauty with high cheekbones and a long, regal neck. Coal-black hair, short and thick with bangs that fell across her forehead and an exotic olive complexion with dark bedroom eyes and full lips. Her large, white shirt fell to her hips and flowed over the top of a pair of sleek black trousers. Sophisticated and most definitely pregnant.

She backed onto the highway and headed east. Not much traffic to worry about today, though he imagined the place swarmed with people from spring break through summer. He'd never been to this part of Alabama before, but now that he had, he'd come back. The sand was sugar white, and when the sun reflected off the water, it turned the Gulf into a brilliant rainbow of greens and blues. There were even dolphins, or so he'd heard. He'd check those out tomorrow.

Tonight, he'd check out a big, isolated house on the beach where a pregnant woman was going to be staying all by herself. Pushing through the door, he jumped into his nondescript sedan and gunned the engine to life. He caught up with the woman's luxury car just as it turned into the supermarket parking lot. Perfect. He needed to pick up a few groceries himself.

Beaches always whet his appetite—for food and excitement. He expected to find plenty of both in Orange Beach.

Chapter Two

Megan fit the key into the lock and opened the front door of Pelican's Roost, feeling better by the minute, even though she'd climbed the wide stairs with a bag of groceries in each hand. The bottom level of the house consisted of a spacious storage area large enough to hold enough beach furniture for at least two dozen guests, an assortment of life jackets, floats and other beach paraphernalia and a seldom-used catamaran. Behind that was parking for up to four cars. The wide steps to the second level were on the outside of the house, and they were the only way to reach the living area of the rambling structure.

Her grandmother had talked for years of adding an elevator to the place, one that carried you straight from the covered parking area into the interior of the house without your having to get out in all kinds of weather or carry shopping bags and groceries up the stairs. She'd never done it, decided in the end that climbing the steps kept her young. Right now, Megan would have loved to have the elevator.

She pushed through the door, and into the high-ceilinged family room. The room was chilly but welcoming all the same. Tomorrow she'd get someone to deliver wood so that she could build a fire in the massive brick fireplace that took up most of one wall. The opposite side of the room had three sets of sliding glass doors, creating a virtual wall of glass. The drapes were pulled, letting in the late-afternoon glow of the sun and giving the illusion that the Gulf rolled right up to the house itself. Already the sight of the water made her feel calmer. Coming here had been the right thing to do.

She shut the front door behind her and headed for the kitchen. Setting a bag of groceries on the counter, she looked around the room and had the distinct feeling her grandmother might walk in any second. The room was filled with memories... Baking cookies with her grandmother. Icing cupcakes and eating more of the gooey concoction than she put on the little cakes. Cutting strips of red and green construction paper and gluing them into chains to drape about the Christmas tree.

The jangling of the phone broke into her thoughts. She picked up the extension by the sink, wondering who'd be calling her so soon after she'd arrived. "Hello."

"I see you made it."

"John. I should have known it would be you. Don't tell me there's already an emergency. I was in the office this morning."

"Rumblings in the merger deal. Boynton wants us to guarantee to keep seventy percent of their management-level people."

"Stick to the fifty percent we offered them. If they weren't so top heavy, they wouldn't have to merge in the first place. Too many chiefs do not make for a good bottom line."

"And if they won't go along with that?"

"They will. Cullecci will make a fuss, but he has his

orders. He'll work with you. Play hardball with the retirement plan, too. What we have at Lannier is far more reasonable and fair then what they've provided. And, John, in case you've forgotten, I'm on leave.''

"How could I forget? Could this pregnancy come at a more inconvenient time?''

"I hope you're not asking me that question.''

"Sorry. I know this is harder on you than on anyone else. Did you contact the adoption agency?''

"Not yet.''

"Don't you think it's time?''

"I'll call them.''

"Good. I don't want you to waste any more time on this than is absolutely necessary. We have too much on our plate. You keep doing the job you've been doing, and you'll be the youngest vice president Lannier's ever had.''

"Do you guarantee that?''

"No, but I can tell you that the new CEO is extremely impressed with you. I had dinner with him last night at Commander's Palace, and he was singing your praises about the way you're handling this acquisition.''

"Don't worry. I'll be back to work in January and the baby will be in her new home.''

"Then we're on the same page. Now take care of yourself,'' he said sincerely. "By the way, Lufkin called from the London office. He want's to know if the meeting is still on for January 12.''

"It's on. I already have my plane reservations.''

"Then just call me if you need anything.''

"Notice I am *not* offering you that same option.''

When she finally hung up, stabbing little pains had started building around her temples. She loved her job, but it was demanding and hectic and all-consuming. And working so closely with a man she'd practically left at the altar added an extra layer of tension to the job. She needed this break, needed time to think and to relax and to grieve for the mother of the baby she was carrying.

In all honesty, she'd had her doubts when her best friend had come to her and asked her to carry her child. But how could she say no when Jackie and Ben wanted the baby so desperately? Nine months of inconvenience for her, a lifetime of happiness and dreams come true for them.

Only now there was no Jackie. No Ben. No parents for the baby that kicked and slept and curled into a tiny ball just below her heart.

Her hands shook as she took the carton of eggs from the paper bag and placed them in the refrigerator. Cheese, crackers, canned soup, fruit juices, cereal. She put them away, sliding the canned goods into empty cupboards that would have been filled to overflowing if her grandmother were still alive.

The old house seemed to close in around her as she worked. As soon as she put the last item away, she opened one of the doors to the balcony and took a deep breath. The smell of saltwater filled her nostrils, and all of a sudden she couldn't wait to walk down to the water's edge and let the incoming surf wash over her feet and pull the shifting sand from beneath her toes.

It was almost dark, but if she hurried, she could watch the final plunge of the sun as it sank into the Gulf. At least that's what it appeared to do, and when Megan was a child, her grandmother had had a difficult time convincing her otherwise. Pulling on a light jacket, she hurried down the front stairs in bare feet, moving faster than she had in days.

THE SUN SET in minutes, but Megan was not nearly ready to go back inside. Bending over, she rolled up the legs of her black pants so that she could walk at the water's edge.

The beach seemed to belong to her tonight. She could see lights from some of the high-rise condos in the distance and the flickering beam of a fishing boat a mile or so out from the coast, but there was not another soul in sight.

That's why she loved December at the beach. The sandy shores were isolated except for the few determined souls like her grandmother who lived here year-round and a few tourists who dribbled in.

Isolated. The word echoed in her mind, and for a second that same unsetting shudder she'd felt this afternoon in the souvenir shop rolled over her. She forced it away. This wasn't the city, and she'd walked this beach alone day or night for as long as she could remember. Her grandmother did the same right up until her heart had given out at the age of eighty-eight.

The events of the past month played in her mind. A horrible accident. A deadly explosion. Jackie and her husband both killed instantly. She'd never forget where she was and what she'd been doing when she got the news. Never forget the shock and, finally, the cold hard realization that she would never see her friend again. The knowledge that the baby growing inside belonged to no one.

She turned back to the house, suddenly chilled and tired and ready to curl up with a cup of hot soup in hand. But she wasn't alone anymore. A lone man was jogging along the beach in her direction, kicking up water and sand as he ran. He was only a few yards away now, and his body took shape. Lean, strong legs, short hair. Familiar. He slowed and her heart raced as she realized he was the man who'd come into the shop while she and Penny were talking.

"Nice night for the beach," he said, stopping a few feet in front of her.

"Yes." Her mouth was dry, but she was being ridiculous. The man had every bit as much right to be here as she did. It was the overactive hormones of pregnancy. "It's warm for December."

"I wondered about that. It's my first time in this area." His gaze traveled to her bulging stomach. "I noticed you in one of the shops this afternoon."

She rested her hands on her stomach. "It would be hard not to notice me."

"Is the baby due soon?"

"The end of the month."

"Do you live here, or are you visiting, too?"

"I'm visiting." That was about as vague as she could manage, short of telling him it was none of his business.

"I jogged by several private homes, but most of them looked dark. I guess a lot of people close up and go home for the winter. It seems a shame, if the winters are always this mild."

"It gets cold sometimes. It just doesn't stay cold."

"It's gorgeous now, but the place sure looks deserted." He let his gaze settle on her face, but his feet shifted restlessly. "Look, if I'm out of line just tell me, but I overheard you tell your friend you were here by yourself. I am, too. Maybe we could have dinner together one night. You seem to know the area, I have no clue where to find the best food."

"I'm very busy." Her tone was sharper than she'd intended, but even if he wasn't dangerous, the man was definitely overstepping his bounds.

"Oops. I offended you. Believe me, I was not trying to

pick you up. I've never been good at that anyway. You can see why." He extended a hand. "Let me start over. My name's Bart Cromwell."

She took his hand but didn't offer her name.

"I'm staying just up the beach, so we'll probably run into each other from time to time. If you change your mind about dinner, let me know. Otherwise, I promise not to bother you."

"I hope you have an enjoyable stay."

"You, too. I'll see you around." He started to walk away, then stopped. "Take care, and if you're staying in a big old house all by yourself as your friend said, you need to lock your doors tight. This seems like a safe little area, but you just never know."

Her thoughts exactly. She picked up her pace as she started back toward the house. A nice-looking man, on the beach alone in December, stopping to ask an extremely pregnant woman out to dinner. Something was seriously wrong with this picture. And he needn't worry. She would lock and bolt every door tonight.

MEGAN STRETCHED OUT on a slip-covered lounge chair in an alcove that looked out over the Gulf. It was her favorite spot in the whole house, a small, cozy room with a large window that provided a marvelous view of the gulf. She had an avalanche of pillows behind her, a knitted throw pulled over her feet and a cup of hot herb tea on the table beside her. All the essentials for relaxing—only she wasn't.

She'd walked every room of the rambling house, even climbed to the cupola above the third floor and checked the doors to the widow's walk. Every door and window was locked tight, but still the uneasiness persisted.

Was it hormones, paranoia brought on by the recent

tragedy, or reasonable caution that wouldn't let her put the stranger on the beach out of her mind? A year ago she'd probably have been intrigued if the rugged, sexy man had tried to pick her up on the beach.

But a year ago it would have made a lot more sense. A year ago she'd been thirty, not pregnant and a perfect size eight. But maybe the guy was gay and didn't care what she looked like. Or maybe he was hungry and only wanted to know where the best places were to eat. It could even be that he was lonely.

Or maybe not.

She walked to the kitchen and retrieved the phone book from the second drawer of the cabinet. It wouldn't hurt to call the local police department and check to see if there had been any problems in the area in recent weeks.

She found the number and punched it in, using the wall phone in the kitchen. The woman who took the call put her on hold and then transferred her to someone else.

"Yes, ma'am, how can I help you?"

The Alabama drawl was unmistakable. Just the familiarity of it eased her fears a little. "I'm staying in a private home on the Gulf in the Orange Beach area."

"Glad to have you. Are you having some kind of problem?"

"No, but I'm here alone, and I was just wondering how safe it is in this area."

"Exactly where are you?"

"Are you familiar with the Lancaster house?"

"Pelican's Roost? Sure am. Hey, is this Megan?"

"Yes. Do I know you?"

"I reckon you do. Class of '88. Hey, hey, hey."

"Roger Collier?"

"The one and only."

Talk about a blast from the past. They had gone to high

school together, but it had been two years since she'd seen or heard from Roger. He'd looked her up when he'd been job hunting in New Orleans, but she hadn't been able to help him. Still, it was good to hear his voice now.

She'd had a terrific crush on him for most of her junior year, but he'd been going steady with Jackie at the time. She'd dated him for a while after he and Jackie broke up, but had broken up with him after a few dates. The only time she'd gone out with him after that had been to the senior prom, when neither of them were dating anyone steady. "How have you been?"

"Terrific. Still single and hanging easy. Will you be in town long?"

"I'm not sure."

"Everybody's been wondering what you were going to do with that place since your grandmother passed away. If you fixed it up a bit, you could probably sell it for a mint of money. Beach property's like gold these days."

"That's what I hear."

"Anyway, good to have you back. Now, what's this about trouble?"

"I ran into a man on the beach when I was out walking just after sunset and he stopped to talk to me. To make a long story short, he made me a little nervous."

"Did he say something out of the way?"

"Not really."

"Was he drunk?"

"No."

"Just a ragged old beach bum, huh?"

"Not that either." Now she felt foolish. "It's nothing I can put my finger on. He just made me a little nervous and I thought I'd see if there had been any trouble in the area."

"The usual stuff. Kids throwing bottles on the beach,

getting loud and rowdy, but we haven't even had a complaint of that since the summer crowd left.''

"I'm sure it's nothing."

"Yeah. You know how it is on the beach. The setting breaks down barriers. People who wouldn't speak to you in town stop and chat. I can send someone out to take a look around if you like, but if he was just out jogging, I doubt they'd find him.''

"No. I'm sure it's nothing," she repeated.

"Probably just a guy looking for a good time. Orange Beach is the safest place in the country. But I'll be here all night. If you change your mind about having an officer come by and check out the house, just let me know.''

"I appreciate that."

They talked a few more minutes about people they both knew from high school. It always surprised her that so many of her classmates still lived in Orange Beach. It had never occurred to her to settle here, but then this had never really been her home. No place had. She'd only lived here her last two years of high school while her mother lived in Spain with her third husband.

The baby kicked as she started up the stairs. So alive, so much a part of her and yet not a part of her at all. She'd carry it for one more month, and then... And then she'd give it up to strangers.

Pushing open the door, she stepped into the bedroom that had been hers for as long as she could remember. The bed was made, the coverlet pulled back to reveal crisp white sheets and fluffy pillows. All it had taken was one call to Fenelda and the house had been readied for her return. The furniture dusted, the cobwebs brushed from the corners, the wooden floors swept clean and the carpets vacuumed. And all six bathrooms had fresh towels on the racks.

Crossing the moss-colored carpet, she opened one of the sliding doors. When she'd been young, the sound of the surf had always served as an unending lullaby, soothing her to sleep almost before she had time to say her prayers. Tonight might be more of a challenge.

She turned off the light in the bedroom, and let the moonlight provide the illumination as she slipped out of her clothes. With the light off, she could see the outline of the thatched-roof gazebo that sat between the house and the beach, see the swing beneath it swaying in the wind. All peaceful.

The moon ducked behind a cloud. She looked away and took a robe from the closet. When she turned back, her heart slammed against her chest. Someone was out there, standing just past the gazebo. All she could see was the outline of a body, but she could picture the man she'd seen earlier on the beach, imagine him watching her house, knowing she was there alone.

A second later the figure headed off down the beach and out of sight. The baby picked that time to give her a swift kick. She splayed her hands across her stomach. "Don't worry, little one. I'm not off the deep end, not yet anyway. Just a little paranoia playing games with my overwrought nerves." Turning away from the balcony, she headed for her bath.

December 5

MEGAN WOKE to the jangle of bells, but it took her a few seconds to realize that it was actually the doorbell and not part of her weird dream. She'd been running across the sand, her feet sinking into it, slowing her down so that whatever she was chasing stayed just beyond her reach.

The bell chimed again. She stretched, kicked out from under the covers and eased her legs over the side of the bed, combing the carpet with her feet until she located her slippers. Grabbing her robe, she tied it around her loosely and headed down the steps, wondering who in the world would come calling this time of the morning.

One peek through the peephole and she breathed a sigh of relief. She should have known Sandra Birney would waste no time coming by to check on her.

She swung the door open, pushing her long dark bangs off her forehead as she did and realizing that she probably looked a total mess. "Come in."

"I will, as soon as I get a look at you." She scrutinized Megan from the top of her head to her toes. "My, you are pregnant."

"I told you."

"I know, but I just couldn't picture it." Sandra brushed past her and set a cloth-topped basket that smelled of cinnamon and nutmeg on the table, before she came back to offer a hug. Southern women always hugged.

"I want to hear everything about the pregnancy, especially how you let someone talk you into it. Will the biological parents be here for the birth?"

"No. I'm going to deliver all by myself—just me and Dr. Brown, and maybe Santa Claus."

"And me. You know I'll be there."

"You like suffering, do you?"

"I don't mind, as long as it's not mine," she teased. "And I love babies."

Megan started the coffee while Sandra caught her up on news of the happenings in Orange Beach. The high-school football team had won the regional playoffs, the elementary-school principal had retired and the Baptist church was building a new sanctuary.

Megan excused herself to go to the bathroom and brush her teeth while the coffee finished perking. She ran a comb through her hair as well and washed her face. The questions would start as soon as they sat down to coffee and muffins, but everything was under control. She had her story down pat, the details worked out so that no one would suspect that the baby she carried belonged to Jackie Brewster, not even the intuitive Sandra Birney.

The delightfully plump and rosy-cheeked grandma was the same age as Megan's mother. They'd gone all through school together, had both been cheerleaders and on the homecoming court. And that was where the similarities ended. Sandra had married her high-school sweetheart and was still married to the man. Her life centered around community events and her children and grandchildren, and she'd stayed close to Megan's grandmother, done the things for her a daughter would have done, had her daughter ever been around. Megan's mother marched to a totally different drummer.

By the time Megan returned to the kitchen, the coffee had been poured into crockery mugs and the muffins set in white dessert plates bordered with a seashell pattern.

Sandra stood at the open refrigerator. "Would you like butter and jam with your muffin?"

"I would love it, but I wouldn't dare. I'll never get down to my normal weight again as it is."

"Then I'll just pour us a little half-and-half for the coffee." She joined Megan at the table with the sugar bowl and a pitcher of milk in hand. "Now, I can't wait to hear all about this baby. Is it a boy or a girl?"

"It's a girl." That was the easy question.

"Who are the lucky parents? They must be very dear friends."

"They are. The mother is a woman I work with. Medical problems prevented her from carrying her own child, and since she wanted a baby so desperately, I agreed to do this for her."

Megan's mind wandered back to the moment when Jackie had first come to her. She'd said no at first, but the look of disappointment in Jackie's face had nearly killed her. It was as if Megan had taken her friend's dreams and stamped them into the ground.

Jackie had already had three miscarriages and the doctor had told her that to try again would be exceedingly dangerous due to her increasingly serious problems with diabetes. Yet Megan had feared that if she said no, Jackie would have gotten pregnant in spite of the doctor's warnings. As it turned out, it wouldn't have mattered anyway.

Sandra swallowed a bite of muffin. "So when the baby's born, you'll just give it to its real parents?"

"That's the plan." Or at least it had been. This was the part she couldn't share with Sandra. Talking about it was painful. Even thinking about it seemed traitorous and cruel, as if she was considering throwing away a part of herself and all that was left of Jackie.

Sandra reached over and took her hand and squeezed it. "I always said you had a heart the size of the gulf. You proved me right again. What does Marilyn think of this?"

"Mother doesn't know. I haven't seen her since I made the decision to have the baby."

"And you didn't want her input. You are wise as well as big-hearted. Where is your mother now?"

"Living in an oceanfront estate in Acapulco with a new husband, a man who owns a chain of luxury resorts. She insists I come down for a visit. I haven't made it yet."

"Is this the man she was telling me about when she came to your grandmother's funeral?"

"That's the one."

"She showed me his picture. He's very handsome."

"And rich."

Sandra sighed. "Of course. Otherwise he wouldn't have stood a chance with her. She learned her lesson when Bob Gilbert stuck her with all his debts."

"Husband number three was definitely an eye-opener for her," Megan agreed.

"She might as well hook up with rich men since she can get anyone she wants. I don't know how she manages it, but she's still as beautiful as the day she was crowned Miss Alabama. We all threaten to lock up our husbands when she comes to town."

"That's my mom."

"Does this make husband number five?"

"Six, I think. You probably missed the French diplomat. He only lasted about six months."

Sandra shook her head, but a smile curled her lips. "That woman. She never fit into Orange Beach. I miss her, though. I still remember when she danced in that play on Broadway. A bunch of us flew up to see her and she got us front-row seats and took us to a cast party. Even in that crowd, she stood out. She was always bigger than life."

Megan nodded but kept her thoughts on that to herself. Her mother was all those things, and if Megan hadn't been her daughter, she might have appreciated it the way Sandra did. But it had never been easy being the daughter of a woman who was bigger than life.

They finished the coffee and muffins, and Sandra left after exacting a promise from Megan that she'd come over for dinner soon. Thankfully, there had been no more questions about the baby. Evidently, Sandra had picked up on her hesitancy to talk about it. But it was better that at least that much was out in the open. It would keep the locals from going nuts trying to find out who had knocked her up.

IT WAS ONE-THIRTY in the afternoon when Megan pulled into the parking lot of the Pink Pony. After Sandra had left that morning, she'd dressed and gone for a long walk on the beach. The sun was bright, the sand warm and the water had sparkled like diamonds. It was the perfect cure for the tinges of fear that had coiled around her last night. And there had been no sign of Bart Cromwell.

Now she was starving, craving an oyster po' boy. Most of the time she tried to eat healthy for the sake of the baby and to curb her weight gain, but the first full day back in town she simply had to have fried oysters.

She took a seat by a window overlooking the Gulf. A couple of young lovers were walking hand in hand along the beach and a man and golden retriever were wading in the water. She didn't bother looking at a menu. She knew what she wanted.

The door opened and a man walked in alone. She recognized him before he even turned around. The broad shoulders, the easy swagger, the faded baseball cap.

When he turned and saw her, his blue eyes lit up and his lips spread into a broad grin, as if they were old friends.

The troubled, anxious feeling that she'd experienced last night hit again, this time with overwhelming force. The man was following her, and there was no logical, innocuous reason for his doing so.

He walked over and tipped his hat. "We've got to stop meeting like this. But since we did, mind if I join you? I hate eating alone."

Chapter Three

The man stood by her table, cap in hand. "If you don't want company, I'll understand."

Her gut instinct was to tell him to keep moving, but she knew that talking to him might be the best way to put aside any irrational fears she had about him. "Please, have a seat."

"Thanks. I went to the tourist center like you suggested. Loaded up on maps, booklets, even money-saving coupons. This place was highly recommended for lunch. I understand they have good gumbo here."

"I haven't tried it, but I'm sure it's good."

He gazed out the large bay window. "It's a great view."

"Did you say that this was your first trip to this area?"

"Yes, ma'am."

"So what made you decide to come now, especially in the off-season?"

"I came down from Nashville to go to my sister's wedding in Mobile. My new brother-in-law suggested I come down here and enjoy some beach bumming and fishing since I had some vacation time left that I needed to use before the end of the year. So here I am."

Here he most definitely was. So far she'd run into him

three times in two days. Now she was sitting across the table from him and still she was picking up strange vibes. Maybe it was because his manner and his motives didn't really match.

His appearance and demeanor suggested an easygoing personality, but when he looked at her, his gaze was intense, as if he was studying her. He had a magnetism about him, a kind of rugged masculinity that would have gone better with a leather motorcycle jacket than the windbreaker he was wearing.

The waitress came and took their order, then returned a minute later with draft beer for him and a glass of milk for Megan. He lifted his glass in a toast.

"To sun, sand and catching fish," he said, clinking his glass with hers. "And to an easy birth and a healthy baby."

"I'll drink to that."

"So when's the little rug rat due?"

"December 27."

"Wow. Hope that stork doesn't get run over by eight tiny reindeer. You must be getting excited with the date so close. Is this your first child?"

"It's my first pregnancy." It was much easier to stick to the truth minus unnecessary facts.

"Well, you look great. I guess it's true what they say about women glowing when they're carrying a child."

It was an idle compliment, the kind she hated. She didn't look great. She looked like a beached whale, and having some stranger tell her differently didn't make her feel any better. But it did bother her that he felt he had to offer compliments, as if he was on the make and she was his prospective pick-up.

He took another long draw on his beer, then drummed his fingers on the table. "Are you always this quiet," he asked, "or is it the company?"

"I'm quiet. And it's the company. I don't ordinarily have lunch with strangers."

"I appreciate your making an exception this time, though I guess I kind of forced it on you. To tell you the truth, I expected you to say no."

"I considered it."

"I can still move to another table if you want, but I'd like to stay."

"Why?"

"I told you, I don't like to eat alone." He fingered the edge of the napkin. "And you look as if you could use someone to talk to. I imagine it's tough being all by yourself when you're pregnant, wandering around that big old house all alone. There's not even another house close enough that someone would hear you if you called for help, you know...if you fell or went into labor or something. You should get a dog, a big one for protection, or do you have one already?"

Apprehension swelled inside her. "How do you know which I'm staying in?"

"I was on the beach this morning. I saw you climbing the steps to go inside."

"I can take care of myself. Besides, I won't be alone after today. My husband is coming in tonight." A bald-aced lie, but it made her seem far less vulnerable.

"Really?"

"Yes."

He dropped the subject, but she had the idea he didn't believe her. The waitress appeared with the food and she ate hers quickly, forcing it down though her appetite had vanished. As soon as she finished, she took a ten-dollar bill from her billfold and dropped it to the table.

"This should take care of my part of the bill. Now, if

you'll excuse me, I have an appointment and I don't want to be late.''

He stood, a smile on his lips that softened his features and made him look more mischievous than sinister. ''I did it again. I don't know how I manage to upset you every time we talk, but I do. It's that old foot-in-mouth disease. I have a terminal case.''

''No. It's just that I have a feeling that you're following me, and if you keep it up, I'll notify the police.'' She hadn't meant to be so blunt, but she'd had enough of him. If he was just a friendly tourist, he could think what he wanted about her. If he was dangerous, she'd let him know she wasn't as vulnerable as she seemed.

She felt his gaze on her as she turned and walked away, but she didn't turn back to see. Her hands were trembling by the time she got to her car and tears burned at the back of her eyelids. She blinked repeatedly, determined to keep them at bay. The last time she'd cried had been at Jackie's funeral, and she wouldn't give in to tears just because— because her life seemed to be falling apart and she didn't have the emotional energy to deal with all of it.

Bart Cromwell. Her job. John. Dealing with the HMO. Thoughts of her mother. Memories of her grandmother. The baby that grew inside her and belonged to no one, certainly not to her.

So why did she feel such an overwhelming bond to the baby growing inside her? Why did the thought of giving her up for adoption seem to equate with having someone reach inside her chest and rip out her heart?

She climbed into the car, lay her head on the steering wheel and cried.

THE MINUTE SHE WALKED through the door at Pelican's Roost, Megan knew that someone had been there while she was gone. She sensed it the way a woman knows when someone else has cooked in her kitchen or borrowed her makeup. It was the little things, the ones she never thought of when everything was in place but that became conspicuous when they were moved.

The rug by the back door was twisted and scrunched up in the middle instead of lying flat and straight. She always pushed the chair back beneath the table when she got up, but one of the chairs in the breakfast nook was pushed back and sitting at an angle. The hairs on the back of her neck stood on end and fear crawled the corners of her mind and skittered along her nerve endings.

But the anxiety she'd been feeling the past two days didn't mesh with the kind of security she'd always felt in the rambling old house. She took a deep breath and forced her mind to consider the possibilities. The housekeeper had a key. Most likely she'd come by and dropped something off or finished a cleaning task she hadn't gotten to before Megan arrived. That had to be it. She was certain the door had been locked when she left and it was locked when she returned. So, whoever had come in had used a key.

Breathing easier, she walked to the phone and punched in Fenelda Shelby's number. While it rang, she pulled a butcher knife from the block on the counter. She ran her thumb and index finger along the edge, wondering if she'd have the nerve or the presence of mine to use it if a stranger appeared. If he were there even now, watching and waiting. A man like Bart Cromwell.

Only she couldn't blame this on him. He had still been inside the restaurant when she'd driven home. Unless he'd come out while she was crying, and she hadn't noticed. No, she was being macabre. The house had basically been empty for two years and no one had so much as broken a window.

"Hello."

"Hi, Fenelda, this is Megan."

"You sound upset. Is something wrong?"

"No." She struggled to steady her voice. She didn't want the whole town thinking she was going nuts, though she was beginning to consider the possibility herself. "I was out for a while and I got the impression someone was in the house while I was gone. I was just wandering if it was you."

"It wasn't me. Is anything missing?"

"No, nothing like that. Do you know if anyone else has a key to this place?"

"Oh, honey, knowing your grandmother, I wouldn't be surprised if half the town has a key. She was always lending the place out to vacationing relatives of the locals when she took off on one of her trips. That woman was salt of the earth, bless her heart, one of the most generous souls in the world. But I don't have to tell you that."

"Has anyone stayed here since Grandmother died?"

"Not that I know of. No one but you. I've kept watch over the place like I told you I would, but I don't go by there every day. I know I haven't told anyone they could use it. I wouldn't do that without your okay."

"I didn't think so. I was just concerned when I realized someone had been here."

"I don't know nothing about it, hon. It's probably just one of your grandma's friends going by to check on the place. But if you're worried, why don't I send my son over? Leroy will check everything out for you."

"Are you sure he wouldn't mind?"

"I'm positive. He's not doing anything but hanging out in his room with music blaring on the stereo anyway. Was everything okay when you got there? I spent a whole day cleaning. I would have stocked a few groceries, but I had no idea what you'd like.''

"Everything was fine, spotless, in fact. And I stopped at the store on the way in and picked up a few essential grocery items.''

"Okay, you take it easy, honey. Leroy will be there in a few minutes.''

Megan felt better about the situation when she hung up the phone, but the knife was still in her hand. She glanced around the kitchen, then walked into the hall and looked up the imposing staircase. Two levels of living space, and on top of it all a cupola used mostly for storage and to gain access to the widow's walk and the marvelous view it provided. The west side provided a magnificent expanse of the Gulf of Mexico for as far as the eye could see.

A huge house with a million places to hide if someone had reason to. In the dusky aura of sunset, Pelican's Roost took on the appearance of a haunted castle. Shadows climbed the walls of the narrow halls, and the screaming of the wind and creaking and groaning of the floorboards sounded as if the place were inhabited by a family of ghosts.

But it was the bright sunlight of midafternoon now. And she was in Orange Beach, not New Orleans. Still, someone had been inside the house, and she wouldn't truly rest until someone had walked through every room and made sure there were no surprise guests. Her pulse slowed to near normal, but, knife in hand, she decided to go outside and wait for Leroy's arrival.

That's when she noticed a basket of muffins on the table in the breakfast nook. Fenelda must have been right, one of her grandmother's friends had stopped in to welcome her home. Still, she'd feel better if Leroy took a look around.

MEGAN WAITED on the second-floor balcony while Leroy roamed the house. She would have gone with him, but she'd have only slowed him down. He climbed a full flight in the time it took her to maneuver a half-dozen steps. He'd promised to check every closet and under every bed, even to climb to the cupola and make sure no one was hiding among the stacks of storage boxes and old metal trunks.

He had his work cut out for him. Besides the family room and kitchen, there was a dining room, a library, a sewing room, a small office, two bathrooms and a couple of sunny alcoves on the second floor. The third floor consisted of six large bedrooms and four more baths. The house rambled and curved and twisted, giving a beach view and access to a balcony to as many rooms as possible.

In fact, Leroy was gone so long, she would have become worried had it not been for the fact that he sang along constantly to the music from the radio headset that seemed glued to his ears. He'd been polite and didn't seem to mind going through the house, but he obviously didn't think she had a thing to worry about. In fact, he'd laughed when he saw the knife she was holding and assured her he didn't need a weapon.

She dropped to one of the lounge chairs on the balcony, leaned back and closed her eyes as the sun beat down on her and warmed her through and through. The baby shifted and gave a few reassuring kicks. "I know you're still there, sweetie. I couldn't forget you if I wanted to. What do you think of the beach house? When you're older, you can play in the water and build sand castles with moats and crocodiles, and we can buy plastic knights to do battle with the enemies.''

Damn. What was she thinking? This baby would never come to Pelican's Roost. Never play with her in the surf or on the sand. Never be a part of her life at all. She closed her eyes and wished that it was January and that everything was over and done with.

Taking deep breaths, she forced herself to clear her mind of thoughts of the baby and think only of the water, constant, eternal, forever moving with the tides.

''All safe and sound.''

She jumped at the voice, her head jerking from the back of the lounge chair.''

''I didn't mean to frighten you,'' Leroy said, stepping between her and the edge of the balcony.

''I must have fallen asleep.''

''No problem. I just wanted to let you know that I checked the house from top to bottom. You got a leak in one of the faucets upstairs. I'll come back and fix it for you one day next week if you like. It won't take much.''

''I'd appreciate that, as long as you let me pay you.''

''I'm not opposed to taking cash.'' He leaned against the balcony, his shaggy blond hair blowing into his face. ''Mama says you're having another woman's baby for her. That's pretty weird, isn't it? I mean, not a lot of people do that, do they?''

''More than you'd think.''

He nodded. ''Still seems strange. I guess I'll be going, unless you need something else while I'm here.''

''I'd like to pay you for your time and trouble,'' she said, expecting him to say no.

''Whatever.''

She walked to the kitchen and retrieved her wallet. ''Is ten dollars enough?''

"Whatever."

She handed him a five and a ten and walked him to the door. He had Fenelda's coloring, but the deep-set eyes and sunken cheeks must have come from his dad. She barely remembered the man, but she was sure she'd met him a time or two over the years. She'd met Leroy, too, but he was much thinner than she'd remembered, with a kind of raunchy look about him that she hadn't expected in Fenelda's son. She wasn't sure how old he was, near thirty, she'd guess.

Still, he'd done what she asked and she'd rest better for it tonight. She felt a little foolish, but at this point in time, damaged pride was much better than lost sleep.

But she was going to have to get a grip on herself and not let a tall, dark and sexy stranger destroy the level of safety she'd always enjoyed at Pelican's Roost. It was the hormones, she told herself again. What else could it be? She was probably in the safest place in the world.

December 8

MEGAN HUGGED her jacket around her as she strolled along the beach. The day had been warm, but the air had turned cold as the sun set, and now the wind had picked up. It whipped her hair around her face and sent the waves crashing against the sand. But the sky was clear, and the stars seemed so near she felt she could reach up and grab a few to save for a time when she knew what to wish for.

Fortunately there had been no sign of the man she'd come to think of as her dark stranger since he'd joined her for lunch three days ago, though she found herself looking for him everywhere she went. At times, she even felt as if someone was watching her and she always imagined it was him.

One night she'd even dreamed about him, a nightmare that had turned erotic. That was what happened to a woman who hadn't had sex in so long she'd almost forgotten what it felt like. Desire had returned full force in the dream, and after she'd wakened, she'd lain awake for over an hour, imagining what it would be like to make love with the rugged stranger, her body reacting as if his hands were actually on her, caressing and touching her most intimate parts.

There was no accounting for dreams, but in reality, her life in Orange Beach settled into a comfortable routine. A walk in the morning, lunch in some out-of-the-way restaurant, an afternoon spent relaxing and reading, and sunset on the beach.

"The wind's picking up, little one. We'll have howling and whining to entertain us tonight while we sleep. Old fishermen crying about the ones that got away. That's what Grandma used to tell me when I'd complain of the noise."

Standing at the edge of the water, she took a few steps out, stepping into a low wave. She slipped her hand under her loose blouse and stroked her stomach. She was growing larger every day.

Her first appointment with Dr. Brown would be tomorrow, but he already had her records from her doctor in New Orleans. "I guess we better start back, little one. I'm getting hungry."

A bowl of hot soup would taste good tonight. She looked out at the Gulf one last time. The steady cresting and falling was almost hypnotic.

It rocked her into a state where she let herself imagine holding a baby girl in her arms and letting it nurse from her breasts, singing her a lullaby and then tucking her into a white crib.

She was so lost in the thoughts that at first she didn't hear the footfalls on the sand behind her. When she did, she spun around just as someone grabbed her wrists and started dragging her farther into the water. She tried to see who it was, but the man's body was black and his face was covered by a ski mask.

All she knew was that he was strong and she couldn't resist his pull. The cold water rose to her waist and stung her skin, made her breath burn in her lungs. She tried to scream, but he shoved her face into the water.

The salt burned her eyes and throat. She had to get to the surface, had to get air, but he pushed her deeper and deeper. She could hear him cursing now, screaming obscenities. Finally the pressure on her neck and head gave way and she floated to the top. She opened her eyes.

The mask was gone. She could see the man's face in the moonlight. It was him. The dark stranger. She'd been right all along. He'd come to kill her and the baby.

Chapter Four

"Megan. Hold on. I've got you. Just hold on."

The brute was dragging her again. She managed one kick. Her feet scraped against the sand. They were going back to shore, but he was holding her head out of the water. She choked and spit out a stream of water.

"That's the way. Clear your lungs. Here. Let me help." He supported her forehead with his hands while she coughed and sputtered and spit up water. Air rushed into her lungs in a sweeping, caustic sensation, and she grew so dizzy that the man's face blurred and became two.

"Why are you following me? Why are you doing this to me?" The words came out chopped and hoarse. She tried to pull away, but he held her against him.

"Listen, Megan. It wasn't me who tried to kill you, and you better be glad I've been following you. If I hadn't been, you'd be sleeping with the fishes tonight."

"Get away from me. Now." She tried to scream. He stifled her with a broad hand over her mouth.

"Would you just pipe down and listen. I'm an FBI agent and I'm not trying to kill you. I'm trying to keep someone else from doing it. I almost slipped up, big-time."

He was crazy. No one wanted to kill her except this

lunatic. She was weak and her head was pounding, but she had to get away from this man.

"I'm going to take my hand away from your mouth, but don't scream."

She begin to cough again, the taste of seawater making her sick. When she finally stopped coughing, she pushed at him again, only she was trembling and so weak the effort was useless. "Get away from me. Please. Leave me alone."

"I'm afraid I can't do that."

She tried to scream, but again he cut off her cries with his hand over her mouth. "Megan, you have got to listen. I'm not lying. I'm with the FBI. You have to trust me."

He pulled her against his chest and kept her wrapped in his arms. His mouth was at her ear. "You're Megan Lancaster. You work at Lannier. Your supervisor is John Hardison. The baby you're carrying belongs to Jackie Sellers Brewster."

"How do you know these things." She was stunned.

"Because I'm who I say I am."

"Why would you be investigating me?"

"I'm not. I'm investigating the explosion that caused Ben and Jackie Brewster's deaths."

"Please, just let me go back to my house."

"I'll take you back."

Her head was spinning. Nothing he said made sense. She couldn't trust him. He'd tried to kill her. Yet everything he said was true, everything except the part about Jackie and Ben. The explosion had been an accident.

"Just try to relax. I'm going to carry you back to the house and put you to bed. If you need a doctor, we'll call one. But you can't tell anyone that I'm from the FBI or why I'm with you."

"You can't carry me. I'm huge."

"I'll worry about that." He scooped her up in his arms without groaning once. "Now, just relax. You'll be home before you know it."

Relax? Fat chance. She was having a nightmare. She'd wake up in a minute and the dark, *strong* stranger who knew everything about her would evaporate like the steam from her teakettle.

But, for now, she was so tired and still dizzy and a little nauseous. She rested her head against his shoulder. He smelled of seawater and musk. Her hair was dripping wet. So was his. Drops of water rolled down his neck and chest. The wind whipped though her wet clothes, but she was too numb to feel the cold. Or maybe a person didn't feel the effects of weather in a nightmare.

He stopped at the front door of Pelican's Roost. "I'm going to put you on your feet. Hold on to me if you feel weak or dizzy, and give me your key so that I can unlock the door."

She dug deep in her pockets. The key was missing. "I must have lost it in the water."

"Do you have another one hidden somewhere?"

"No."

"I can break a window."

"Don't you dare. Get my cell phone from my car. I'll call the housekeeper and have her come over and unlock the door."

"And then we'll have to come up with a story to explain our being soaking wet."

"You can get out of sight while she's here. I'll tell her I was wading in the surf and fell. As awkward as I am with this body, she'll believe it."

"Let's see if you get her before we work out the details. Breaking the window is no problem, and I can fix it tomorrow."

Only she didn't want him around tomorrow. She leaned against the door as he bounded down the steps and retrieved the phone. A minute later she had Fenelda on the phone.

She said hello but interrupted Fenelda's usual string of small talk. "I lost my key while I was on the beach. I thought maybe you or Leroy would run one over to me."

"No use to do that. There's a key taped under the third step. Your grandmother put it there after she locked herself out a time or two. Check there, and if you don't find one, I'll get Leroy to bring you mine."

She held her hand over the speaker end of the phone and repeated the instructions to Bart. She was shivering now, the cold finally seeping through the shock. Bart showed no signs of the recent ordeal. He bounded down the steps, bent and ran his hand beneath the third step. When he stood up, the key was in his hand, and he gave her the thumbs-up sign.

All her worry about who had a key and there had been one beneath the step all the time. If half the town had a key to this house, the other half probably knew where to find the spare. She'd have the locks changed first thing in the morning.

Bart turned the key in the lock and pushed the door open. When he tried to help her inside, she pulled away from him. "I'm okay."

"I think you should call your doctor, tell him you fell in the surf. See if he thinks you need to go to a hospital and get checked."

"He'll think I need to have my head checked for walking in the surf at eight months pregnant."

"I agree with him, but I've seen you out there, wading almost knee deep."

The man had been watching her every move, following

her, just as she'd thought. She'd have to learn to trust her instincts more. At least it was nice to know she wasn't losing it, falling into a state of stress-induced paranoia.

He held on to her as he walked her to a chair. "How do you feel? Are you having any kind of pains in your stomach?"

"I feel as if I was run over by a truck." She touched her hand to her stomach. "But I'm not having any contractions or unusual stomach pains. And I felt a couple of good strong kicks when you were carrying me back to the house."

"The water probably acted as a support for your body."

"Lucky me."

"You are lucky. You're alive."

Which is more than she could say for Jackie and Ben. The impact of Bart's words finally sank in. She dropped to the wooden rocker in front of the fireplace, the horror and pain she'd felt at hearing of Jackie's death overtaking her as if it had happened all over again. "Why do you think someone murdered my friends?"

"First you need to get out of those wet clothes."

She looked at the stairs and moaned. She wasn't sure she had the energy to climb them.

"Are your clothes upstairs?"

She nodded.

"Why don't you stay in the chair and let me get you a robe?"

And then she'd be forced to entertain the dark stranger in just a robe. Only the wet clothes she had on now were no better. They clung to her, outlining the baby paunch and the tips of her nipples.

"It's in the bathroom—the third door on the right,"

she said, choosing the lesser of two evils. "It's blue. You can't miss it."

He climbed the steps two at a time, probably afraid to be gone long, worried that she'd call the police. Part of her wanted to, but the man's words were taking root in her mind and were starting to make sense. If it had been him who was trying to kill her on the beach a few minutes ago, he'd have had no reason to back off. And if he wasn't with the FBI, how did he know that she was carrying Jackie's baby?

Still, she had lots of questions. And she wanted answers.

"BART."

He looked up from the fireplace and the logs he was lighting as Megan came back into the huge family room. She'd tied a towel around her hair, turban style, and exchanged her wet clothes for the fuzzy blue robe. It stretched over her stomach and fell into loose folds around her ankles.

"I thought I'd build a fire, if that's all right," he said.

"It's perfect. You should change out of your wet clothes, too."

"I'm six feet two inches. I doubt you'd have anything to fit me. Besides, these shorts will dry fast." And he'd already shed his T-shirt to reveal a magnificent chest.

"At least you were dressed for the occasion."

"I'm just glad I had my binoculars on you at the exact moment he attacked."

"Where were you?" she asked.

"Standing in a cluster of sea oats just past your gazebo."

"Do you watch me every time I leave the house?"

"I try," he admitted.

"That's all you do—just watch me?"

"I've had worse jobs, and in a lot worse places. Besides, you've made it fairly easy lately, going to lunch at the same time every day, walking at the same times."

"I'm a creature of habit."

"Most folks are," he added. "The decent ones and the criminals. That's how we trap a lot of them."

"So you followed me here to Orange Beach because you expected someone would try to kill me?"

"We thought it was possible."

"We meaning the FBI?"

"Right." He raked the windblown hair away from his face.

Megan took the towel from her head and began to rub it over the ends of her hair. It looked darker when it was wet, black and shiny. It struck him again how pretty she was and how vulnerable she looked. He'd never guarded a pregnant woman before, never realized that it would affect him the way it had.

A few minutes ago, when he'd seen her fighting for her life, the usual surge of adrenaline had been fueled by a fury he seldom felt anymore. What kind of monster would attack a pregnant woman? A foolish question. He knew this monster and nothing was beyond him.

But pregnant or not, Megan Lancaster was no pushover. She'd fought like a wild woman in that water, and he had the feeling he was going to have a hard time getting her to let him call the shots from here on out. But nobody loved a challenge more than he did.

The sputtering logs caught in a burst of flame, sending fingers of fire up the chimney. He closed the screen and backed away. "That should chase away the chill."

She was standing behind him with a beach blanket. "This might help, too, especially until your clothes dry."

"Great idea." He wrapped it around his shoulders.

"Did you get a good look at the man who tried to kill me?"

"I couldn't be sure. It was dark, and it happened so fast. Once I pulled him off you, he took off before I had a chance to yank that stupid mask from his face."

"Why didn't you go after him?"

"If I had, you would have drowned." He glanced toward the kitchen. "Now we need to think about food. Have you eaten?"

"Not since lunch."

"Good. Neither have I."

The phone rang. She jumped up to get it, but he caught her arm. "Let it ring."

"It's probably my boss. He'll keep calling until I answer."

"John Hardison?"

"Yes."

"Then answer, but don't say anything about what's happened." He read the questions in her eyes, mixed with a tinge of suspicion. That was the one thing he hated about this job—innocent people got caught up in the actions of hardened criminals. "Trust me, Megan. I'll protect you and the baby. You won't get hurt again, but you have to do what I say. Just answer the phone and act as if nothing's wrong."

He listened to her end of the conversation while he rummaged in her cabinets for food. She was eating for two, and he was hungry himself, but his culinary talents were extremely limited. After they ate they'd work out a plan. No more trying to guard a woman in a secluded old beach house. She wouldn't like it, but he was going to stick to her every second of the day and night until the man he was after was behind bars.

Even if it took him right into the delivery room.

MEGAN SAT at the kitchen table, using her spoon to make swirls in the remains of her tomato soup. Bart was on his second bowl and he'd eaten every bite of the BLT sandwich he'd made. She'd only managed to get down half of hers and a few sips of the soup.

It seemed strange to be sitting across the table from the man she'd seen as sinister and frightening up until an hour ago. Now she was buying into his story even though she'd still seen no real proof of who he was.

"I'd like to see your badge," she said, not that she'd know the difference if it was a fake.

"I'll do you one better, I'll give you a number at the bureau. But in the meantime, I'll need to pick up some clothes over at my condo. As big as this place is, I'm sure you have lots of extra bedrooms."

"You can't stay here."

"It's the best solution."

"Not for me."

"You have a short memory, Megan." He glanced at the kitchen clock. "A little over an hour ago, you were fighting for your life. The man ran off, but he's still out there somewhere waiting for his chance to attack again. I'm not planning to leave you alone—not for a second."

"I'll decide that after I have proof you are who you say you are."

He wiped his mouth with the flowered cotton napkin. "Are you always this suspicious?"

"I work in the world of big business. I learned long ago not to trust anything but verifiable facts."

"Good. I'm not a particularly trusting man myself. Now, why don't you call your doctor and then we'll make a little trip to my condo to pack my suitcase."

"You won't need much for one night."

He shook his head. "You still don't get it, do you? I will be with you every second of the day and night from now until the man who tried to kill you is apprehended."

"That won't be necessary. I've had enough of the good life. I'm driving back to New Orleans first thing in the morning." She wasn't sure when she'd made that decision, but right now she couldn't wait to leave Pelican's Roost.

"No. You're staying here."

She stood and glared at him across the table. "FBI or not, Bart Cromwell, you will not tell me what to do and where to live. I'm a citizen, not a criminal."

"Okay." He spread his hands on the table. "I'm not telling you. I'm *suggesting* that you stay in Orange Beach."

"Why? To make it easier for some lunatic to drown me?"

"You're out here in an isolated setting. It's much easier for me to protect you. Besides, this is a small town. We have a much better chance of finding your would-be killer before he has a chance to strike again."

"Why would this man have killed Ben and Jackie, and why would he want to kill me?"

"We don't know. We only suspect that the explosion was rigged and thought the man might follow up by killing their unborn child."

"You don't know more or you're not saying more?"

"I've told you what I can."

This couldn't have anything to do with Jackie. It had to involve Ben. He'd seemed such a nice guy, not that she knew him all that well. Now that she thought about it, she wasn't sure Jackie knew him all that well either. She'd fallen in love with him on a vacation to some island in the Caribbean. They eloped a few months later. She'd never heard her mention Ben's family.

"So you think the man is not after me but after the baby?"

"We think it's possible. That's why I'm here."

Her heart plunged to her stomach. This madman, whoever he was, planned to kill the baby. The ultimate payback to Ben for whatever sin he'd committed in this man's eyes. He'd kill not only Ben, but his wife and his unborn child.

She was exhausted, so tired she could barely stand, and yet something pushed and hardened inside her, a protective surge that was so strong it nullified the fear. Her fingers clutched the back of the chair and she faced Bart. "Tell me what I have to do."

"Does that mean you're willing to stay in Orange Beach?"

"It means I'll sleep on the sand in a hurricane if that's what it takes to stop this lunatic and protect the baby."

"Let's hope it doesn't come to that."

"We need to go to your condo and pick up your things. I want to see your badge and I want to talk to your supervisor. But if this checks out, you just got yourself a partner."

December 9

MEGAN WOKE to the smells of frying bacon, freshly brewed coffee and salty air. She stretched, then groaned as the ache in her arms and legs clamored for attention. She moved slower this time and ran her hand along her stomach.

"Good morning, little one. I smell food. I'm assuming

that means our guest is cooking. He's the same dark stranger I told you about, but I checked all his credentials last night. Apparently he's a real FBI agent and he's here to protect us. The cooking is a bonus. So even though someone roughed us up a little last evening, you don't need to worry about a thing, not until you get ready to come kicking into the world. I hear that's a bumpy ride.''

She, on the other hand, had a few things to worry about. She'd talked to the doctor last night, told him partial truths, and he'd said she was probably fine as long as she didn't have any bleeding or contractions. Still, she was glad she had an appointment scheduled for this afternoon.

And somehow she'd have to deal with living with a man in the house. She was about to slide her feet over the side of the bed when she heard footsteps coming up the stairs. So she pulled the sheet up to her neck and waited for Bart to appear. When he stopped at her door, he had a wicker breakfast tray in hand.

''Don't tell me that's for me,'' she said.

''I figured you deserved it after last night.''

''Are you going to join me?''

''Do you want company?''

''Why not? I think we need to talk about how I'm going to explain your living here for a few days.''

''I have that all worked out.''

He narrowed his eyes and his mouth stretched to the left side. She had the feeling he was about to hit her with something she wasn't going to like, and she didn't want bad news to spoil her appetite again. The baby needed nourishment. ''Have your breakfast before it gets cold. The plans can wait until after we eat.''

She picked up a piece of bacon and nibbled on the end of it as he went downstairs to fix a tray for himself. The bacon was crunchy, just the way she liked it. She washed it down with coffee. For the first three months of the pregnancy, she hadn't been able to drink coffee without getting nauseous, but now it tasted better than ever. Still, she limited herself to one cup a day. Too much caffeine was not good for the baby.

Neither was having a killer chase her. And she had an idea that Bart's plan wouldn't make her feel any better. She'd find out soon enough. In the meantime, she took another sip of coffee and tried to find a way to get close enough to the tray not to spill food all over herself. "No offense, baby, but you do take up a lot of space."

After a few minutes, Bart appeared at the door, and she tried to ready her mind for the next round of surprises from the stranger with a badge.

Chapter Five

Bart set his tray on the table by the window. "This is some layout you have here. The closest I've ever been to living the life of the rich and famous."

"My grandfather built it for my grandmother years ago. He wanted her to have her dream house. She designed it herself, down to the gingerbread trim. It could use some restoration, but it suits me fine the way it is."

"This is a beautiful stretch of land and there are no high-rises nearby to block the view."

"My grandmother said the land was practically worthless back then, nothing but miles of sand. No one ever expected this stretch of beach to build up the way it has."

"I can see why it did. It rivals the Caribbean for sheer beauty."

"Is this really your first trip to the area?"

"It is. You actually caught me in the truth."

"So what do I believe about you? Is Bart Cromwell even your real name?"

"It is for now, and that's about as real as it gets for me. Every assignment I'm a different person with a different background, a different personality. Right now I'm Bart Cromwell, a used-car salesman from Nashville. I can fix you up in a great little low-mileage sedan for less than two hundred dollars a month. Don't worry about your debt. Everybody's credit's good with me.''

"Hey, you are good," she said. "Makes me want to go out and kick some tires and peek under a hood." But in other words, there was no use bothering to get to know him. He would never be who or what he claimed. She spread a layer of orange marmalade on her buttered toast. Whoever he was, he made a good breakfast.

He forked a bite of egg. "There's got to be a dozen rooms in this place."

"I've never counted them, but let's see. There are six bedrooms, countless baths, the big family room where we sat by the fire last night, the kitchen, a library, that little cubbyhole at the top of the stairs on the third floor. There's a treadmill in there in case it's too wet to walk on the beach. And then there's the cupola. It's used mostly for storage now, but when I was a teenager, it was where Jackie and I went to giggle and talk about boys."

"You and Jackie Brewster. As close as two people could be."

"Only she was Jackie Sellers back then."

"Right. Daughter of Janelle and Lane Sellers. But back to the subject of Pelican's Roost. Your grandmother must have known you loved the place when she left it to you free and clear."

"You do know everything about me."

The conversation died as they ate. Bart finished first even though he'd had twice as much on his plate. He didn't appear to have an inch of fat on him, yet his appetite was ravenous. She'd like to find out his secret.

After he drained his coffee, he turned from the window and fastened his piercing blue eyes on her. "Actually, I don't know everything about you, Megan. I only know facts that are in a computer somewhere or that are common knowledge.''

"What else is there to know?"

"Tell me about your relationship with John Hardison."

"He's my associate. We're heading up a merger team together at the present time."

"But you were engaged at one time."

"You didn't leave a stone unturned, did you? Want to tell me how many times we slept together or did that not make it into anybody's data bank?"

"None that I have access to." He leaned in closer. "I'm not into voyeurism, Megan. But my job right now is keeping you safe, and the more I know about you, the easier that will be."

She sighed and stared out the glass door, focusing on the morning sun rays that sent sparkling sprays along the surface of the Gulf. She'd always been a very private person, and knowing that this stranger knew almost as much about her as she did about herself made her extremely uncomfortable. But not nearly as uncomfortable as she'd been last night in the hands of a killer. That left her no choice but to cooperate.

"John and I were engaged, but we broke up over a year ago. Now we're friends and co-workers."

"That must be awkward."

"We're adults. We handle it."

"Is he planning to visit you here at the beach?"

"No. He wasn't invited, not that he would have come anyway. Spending time with a pregnant woman is not his idea of fun."

"Then that's one less person we have to worry about. There's no reason for him to know anything more than what we tell your friends around Orange Beach. Do you plan to stay here until the baby's born?"

"That was my original plan. You seem to be setting up my agenda now."

"Having the baby here will work out fine. Hopefully, this will all be over long before the birth."

"I should certainly think so. That's two and a half weeks from now." She pushed the tray away. "Now, tell me about this plan that you have."

He exhaled sharply as he gave her his undivided attention. "You, Megan Lancaster, are about to knock a man right off his feet and into your bed."

"You, Bart Cromwell, must have crumbled hallucinatory drugs into your eggs."

"No. This is pure genius."

"I assume the guy's blind."

"Twenty-twenty vision. You're looking at him. We'll laugh and hold hands and stare into each other's eyes at local restaurants. We might even be spotted dancing cheek to cheek at one of the clubs."

"Oh, no!" She swung her legs over the side of the bed. "You may only exist in this one moment in time, but I don't. I know people in this town, and I'm not going to become a spectacle. You can be a friend, a renter, or a relative, but I will not pretend to be your lover, not with this body."

He walked over and stood beside her. "What happened to your promise to do whatever it takes to catch the killer."

"Look at me." She stood and clasped her hands beneath her bulging belly. "Even if I agreed to do this, who would believe you're attracted to me? I'm eight months pregnant. I look like a blimp."

"That's only in your mind." He put his hands on her shoulders. "I've thought this through. I need to be with you every time we leave the house, and we have to make our being together look as natural as possible. If it looks like a setup, the man will bide his time. He'll be out there waiting for me to slip up. Waiting to strike again. And neither you nor the baby will be safe.''

She closed her eyes and bit her bottom lip as terror set up camp in her chest and wrapped around her heart. These feelings weren't good for the baby. She had to get hold of herself and stay in control. No one would hurt her baby. Bart wouldn't let them. *She* wouldn't let them.

Her baby. A blunder of the mind. But she couldn't let it happen again. She opened her eyes and concentrated on taking smooth, even breaths. ''We'll do this your way, Bart, but I'm warning you. Don't push it too far. A few laughs. A little hand-holding. You can even look into my eyes as if we're lovers. But this is only for show. When we come back into this house, it's strictly business.''

''That goes without saying.''

''Now, when do the games begin?''

''I'd say over lunch. We have to sell the act as quickly as possible.''

''And once we've convinced the people around here that we're lovers, do we just wait for this madman to strike again?''

''Do you have a better idea?''

''Hardly.'' She raked her long bangs behind her ear, her mind still struggling with the problems his plan encompassed. ''It's not going to work, Bart. No one will believe you came here on vacation and hooked up with a pregnant woman.''

''Actually, we're going to spread the word that I'm an old boyfriend who came here to visit and the sparks just started flying again.''

She shook her head. ''They'll never buy it.''

''Sure they will. I am very good at what I do.''

"I am too, and this isn't it." She stepped around him and walked to the door. "I'm going to shower and get dressed."

He smiled. "Wear something sexy. You've got to knock my socks off."

"Sexy." She put out her hands and gave him the full frontal view of her in her oversize cotton gown. "It would take a miracle for a man to get turned on by this."

He muttered something under his breath that sounded like "You'd be surprised." Obviously she hadn't heard him right.

MEGAN OPENED the top drawer of the antique bureau and took out the small jewelry case she used for traveling. Jewelry was not one of her weaknesses, but she did have a few pieces she enjoyed wearing. The gold bangle bracelet her grandmother had given her before she died would be perfect today. Something sturdy and familiar in a world that seemed to be spiraling out of control.

She opened the case. Her silver and jade watch and gold earrings were there, but not her bracelet.

Strange, she would have sworn she'd brought it with her.

She slipped the earrings into her earlobes, securing the backs without bothering to walk to the mirror. Ready or not...

Wrapping her fingers around the railing, she headed down the stairs for her grand entrance as a pregnant femme fatale. She'd brought mostly maternity pants and oversize shirts with her to the beach, but she had thrown in a couple of dresses and the two-piece outfit she'd decided to wear today. It was a blue jumper dress with tiny pleats down the front and a white broadcloth shirt that went under it.

Sexy was probably the last word she'd have chosen to describe herself, but she did like the way she looked in blue. And she'd put on makeup and brushed her hair into a stylish flounce. Dressed to avoid being killed. Strangely enough, she felt safer with Bart around.

A few days ago he'd been a sinister figure, a man who looked at her with piercing blue eyes and knew that she was staying alone in an isolated beach house. Now he'd moved in.

"Are you ready to go?"

He turned at the sound of her voice and let out a low wolf whistle.

"I told you the performance isn't necessary at home."

"That wasn't a performance. You look very nice today."

"I look very pregnant."

"You do have trouble accepting a compliment. Didn't John ever tell you that you're a beautiful woman?"

"John does not do compliments."

"Then John deserved to lose you. Now, let's go wow the locals."

"It's too early for lunch."

"I was thinking we should start with the grocery store. That's always a good place to run into the neighbors. Drugstores are good, too, and coffee shops, bookstores…"

"I'm still not sure how to handle this."

"Just be yourself, a woman from Orange Beach who's come home for Christmas and to have a baby. How many people around here know it's Jackie's baby you're carrying?"

"I'm counting on the fact that no one knows it. She doesn't have family here any longer, so there's no reason why anyone would know about the surrogate arrangement.

Besides, she had kept it a secret from everyone except a couple of her closest friends. It was a superstition thing. She didn't want anything to jinx her chances at finally becoming a mother.''

"So I'd heard."

"But still, *you* found out about the baby." She planted her hands on the back of the sofa and stared at him. "How did you?"

"From questioning one of her closest friends. A neighbor."

"I will never feel that any part of my life is private after this."

"It's not that bad."

"Maybe not from your side of the playing field."

"So, do you want the people around town to believe that this is your baby?"

"No way. I'm telling anyone who asks that I'm a surrogate parent, the same as I did in New Orleans. But only John knows that it's Jackie's baby. I let him in on the plan in a weak moment when I was still deciding whether or not to honor Jackie's request."

"Fine. We'll leave it at that. No one needs to know anything else."

He took her arm as they walked down the front steps. "You'd probably be more comfortable if we take your car. I'll drive if you like, but I don't have to. I'm not one of those macho guys who can't handle sitting in the passenger seat when a woman's at the wheel."

"You can drive. I barely fit behind the wheel."

"Just tell me where to go."

On the one hand, she was tempted to do just that. On the other, it was kind of nice having a man around for a change, even if he was only playing the role of adoring lover. Actually, he did a better job of it than John ever had.

The man was good. She'd give him that. And sexy as hell.

JOHN HARDISON SAT at his desk, pushing a pencil around and wishing Megan was here to handle her share of the workload. The whole situation was ridiculous. An extremely competent professional deciding to become the surrogate mother for some girl she went to high school with.

He knew from the beginning it would be a mistake, tried to warn her. But as usual, she hadn't listened to him. Instead, she'd stretched a perfect body into an ungodly shape.

She'd broken off with him because she wasn't ready for commitment. Yet if putting her whole life on hold for a baby that wasn't even hers wasn't commitment, he'd like to know what was. But none of that worried him as much as the possibility that she might be planning on keeping this baby instead of giving it up for adoption.

He'd always thought they'd end up together someday, but damned if he was going to take on a stranger's child. As far as he was concerned, Megan keeping this baby would mark the end of any possibility of their getting back together. And he had no intention of sitting by and doing nothing while that happened.

"There's a long-distance call for you from a Mr. Cullecci with Boynton Drilling and Exploration. Do you want to take it?"

He snapped out of his reverie at the sound of his assistant's voice. "Put him through."

But he wasn't finished with this baby business. Not by a long shot.

BART PUSHED the buggy down the meat aisle. He usually wasn't into kitchen duties, but cooking at the beach seemed more like fun than work. He stopped and picked up a cellophane-wrapped package. "These porterhouses look good. What do you say to grilled steak for dinner?"

"Are you cooking?"

"Yeah. I noticed there's a grill out back. You can sip wine and watch the sunset while I fix dinner."

"You're on, all except the wine. I'll settle for mineral water with a squeeze of lime."

"That's right. I almost forgot. Alcohol is off limits for pregnant women." He dropped the steaks into the basket. "Do you miss it?"

"Occasionally. I'm what people refer to as a cheap drunk. Two drinks and I turn into a chatterbox, but I like a glass of wine now and then or a margarita."

"A chatterbox. I'll have to come back for a visit when you're not pregnant."

"You can't. You'll be Jack Smith, truck driver, living in Montana by then."

She leaned over and picked out a package of boneless chicken breasts. He scanned the aisles. No sight of the man he was looking for in the store, but even killers had to eat and he was sure the man was around here somewhere.

He spied a saucy blonde rounding the corner. He recognized her at once. "Don't look now, sweetheart, but we're about to have our first customer."

Megan spun around, one hand on the basket, the other still clutching a package of chicken. "Oh, no. It's Penny Drummonds. I knew this wouldn't work. She's the woman I was talking to that first day in the souvenir shop."

"I remember."

"You would. But the point is, she knows I didn't know

you, so how could you be an old boyfriend?'' she whispered as Penny was heading toward them, her eyes open wide.

"Megan, I'm glad I ran into you. I've meant to call you, but you can't imagine how hectic it is running after two kids.'' She turned her full attention to Bart. "Are you two together?''

He put a hand on Megan's shoulder. "Yeah, we are. Have we met before? You sure look familiar.''

Megan looked at him as if he'd lost his mind, but didn't jump into the conversation.

Penny sidled closer. "I talked to you in that shop across the highway the other day. It was the same day I ran into Megan, but you two didn't seem to know each other then.''

"I remember you now. You were looking at running shorts.''

"Right.'' She still eyed them suspiciously. "How did you two meet?''

"We met years ago, back at Auburn. I gave Megan a call when I knew I was going to be down this way for my sister's wedding, and she told me to come by the house. Then I ran into her in the store and didn't even recognize her. Of course, the last time I saw her was back in college. She had long hair and—''

"And I was a lot smaller,'' Megan added, finally jumping into the conversation.

"Imagine my surprise when I got to her door and realized she was the same person I'd walked right past in the souvenir shop.''

Penny's eyebrows arched. "So you two are old friends?''

"That's right,'' Megan said, trying hard to lie without blushing.

"Actually, we were a little more than friends," Bart said. "Even then I knew a good thing when I saw one."

Penny smiled. "You know, Megan, I told Tom you were in town and he said he'd love to see you. Why don't you and—" She looked at him questioningly.

"Bart Cromwell." He extended a hand.

She took it and held it while she finished her invitation. "Why don't you and Bart come over on the sixteenth? We're having some friends over for a holiday get-together. Nothing fancy."

"I'm not making plans these days, Penny."

"I understand. You could even be in the hospital by then, but the invitation's open in case you can make it."

Bart watched Megan as she talked with Penny. Suspicious, intelligent and pregnant, she was the woman who'd lead a vicious killer into his trap. Two days ago she'd been only a name on a file, a picture on his computer screen, a woman carrying a dead man's baby. He needed to keep it that way. Only, there was some nebulous quality about her that was crawling under his skin.

Whatever it was, he'd control it. He was a professional and he'd never wanted to capture any man the way he wanted to capture The Butcher.

Old images flickered in his mind. Blood, bodies, a teddy bear still clasped in a lifeless hand. But The Butcher walked the streets a free man, doing the only thing he knew how to do. Kill. And kill again.

Stabs of guilt punched him in the gut. He was keeping vital information from Megan, but she was on a need-to-know basis, and she did not need to know the identity of the killer. He'd protect her and he'd get his man. So why did he feel like such a rat? He was dealing with a pregnant woman that was getting to him. It changed his MO, softened his rough edges so that he barely recognized himself.

"You handled that amazingly well," Megan said when Penny finally walked away.

"Yeah. We've been seen. Let's get out of here."

"Is something wrong? I expected you to be gloating."

"Later. Right now, I'd like a cold drink and a seat in the sunshine overlooking the beach."

"I know just the place."

THIS TIME Megan took the wheel of her car and drove back to Pelican's Roost. They needed to put the steaks and chicken in the refrigerator, and the second-story balcony was the perfect place to help Bart deal with the dark mood that had come over him. She hadn't asked him any more questions, but if he'd spent his adult life dealing with the type of man who'd tried to drown her last night, then she imagined he had lots of ghosts to deal with.

There was a dark green pickup truck parked in the driveway as they drove up, spattered with mud and rusted in spots.

"Looks like you have company," Bart said. "Do you recognize the truck."

"No."

"Then leave your car parked right behind it." He pulled a gun from under his jacket, a black pistol with a glint of brass on the handle. The sight of it changed the sunny day to an ominous gray blur, but she did as he said.

Before she'd cut the engine, Leroy Shelby came strolling around the side of the house, barefoot, shirtless and wearing a pair of tattered jeans. "It's okay. That's Leroy Shelby, the housekeeper's son," she said. "Please, don't let him see the pistol."

She stepped out of the car. "Leroy, what are you doing here?"

"I came by to fix that leaky faucet I told you about. Sorry it took me so long."

The leaky faucet. She'd forgotten all about it. "I didn't recognize your truck."

"I was in Mom's car when I came by the other day. The truck only runs about half the time. It's just waiting on me to save enough money to give it a decent burial."

She introduced Bart to Leroy and realized Bart was sizing him up the way he likely did everyone he met when working on a case. Leroy looked a little unkempt and apparently lacked ambition, but as far as she knew he'd never been in any real trouble. "Have you already fixed the faucet?"

"I would have, but someone moved the key that's usually taped under the front steps."

"I moved it," Megan said. "I'm a little uncomfortable with it being there. From now on, you'll need to get a key from your mother before you come by."

"No problem."

Bart took her arm. "Actually, since Leroy and I are staying here for a while, it might be best to call before you come by."

"Whatever."

Megan could only imagine what Fenelda would think when she got that piece of information. She'd likely decide Megan had turned into her mother after all.

Bart made small talk with Leroy as they started toward the house, and by the time they reached the front door they were laughing together like old friends. Of course, everyone was an old friend to Bart Cromwell. The man only existed until this job was complete. Then he became a different person in a different town with a different woman on his arm.

Pity the woman who fell for him, and that would be

easy to do if she brought his concern as real, his touch as genuine. Strong yet gentle, mysterious yet intimate enough to bring a pregnant woman breakfast in bed.

"Now I'm really ready for that cold drink." Bart said when Leroy had left them to go to the leaky faucet. "If you stake out two seats on the balcony, I'll fetch and carry. Fruit juice, milk or water?"

"Apple juice, on the rocks."

"You got it." He opened the cabinet and pulled out a juice glass.

"A woman could get spoiled if she stayed around you too long."

"I can't recall any woman ever saying that about me before." He dropped a couple of cubes of ice into the glass and filled it with juice. "Either you spoil easily or you bring out a trait in me that usually stays under wraps."

"I'm sure it's the pregnancy," she said, keeping her tone light. "You probably feel as if you have to wait on me."

He slipped the glass into her hand. Their fingers touched as she fit hers around the base, but neither of them pulled away. When she looked up, their gazes met and held, and a slow traitorous warmth crept through her.

"The fact is that your being pregnant affects me, Megan. I won't deny that, but if you think it works as some kind of shield to make you less desirable, you're wrong."

His words tiptoed around feelings she didn't want to deal with, couldn't afford to experience. Finally, he pulled his hand away, breaking the touch, but not the sensual tension that had burned between them.

She walked to the balcony and stood staring at the Gulf.

Only this time its waters held no curative powers. She was still standing there when Bart stepped up behind her.

"When you're not Bart Cromwell, when you're whoever it is that's on your birth certificate, do you have a wife?"

Chapter Six

Bart stood in the sunshine staring out on a world that looked a lot like he'd imagine paradise would look, and dealt with a question that reminded him of hell.

"Is that important, Megan?"

"Maybe not, but my life is in your hands. I feel I need to know something about you, the real you, not some fake identity that you become at will. I want to know if the man I'm pretending to be falling for has a wife and children. I want to know if you ever just lead a normal life, if you have feelings beyond what your job dictates."

"I don't have a wife or children. I'm divorced, but I'm not a robot. I feel hurt and pain and heartbreak just like the next guy. When I'm cut, I bleed. But I carry out my duties the best way I know how, and that means following bureau policy. For this case, I'm Bart Cromwell, car salesman from Nashville, Tennessee."

"You know everything about me, and I know nothing about you. I'm not sure I like the bureau's M.O."

"I don't always like it myself. I still follow it."

His cellular phone rang, a welcome break from the tension that had developed between them. He pulled it from the holder at his waist and took the call. "Cromwell," he said, staying in character. "What's up?"

"I've got good news."

"Hold on a minute." Bart walked back through the open door and into the kitchen. He didn't need Megan to hear the rest of this conversation. He lowered his voice as much as he could and still be heard. "Did you spot Caraway?"

"No. I've had no luck at all. Neither has Paul, and we've covered the Orange Beach area like fleas on a dirty dog. But rumor has it that an informant reported seeing him last night outside a bar in St. Louis."

"No way."

"He's a reliable informant."

"Joshua Caraway was not in St. Louis last night. I told you in our last conversation that he attacked Megan on the beach and tried to drown her."

"Not if the informant's on target, and from all accounts, the man's dependable."

"Then how do you explain the attempt on Megan Lancaster's life?"

"I don't have to explain it. If it wasn't Caraway, the attack would fall under the jurisdiction of the local police. Our job is to track down Joshua Caraway and get him back to prison before he makes good on the threats he made eight years ago."

"Trusted informant or not, they will not find Joshua Caraway in St. Louis. He's behind the attack last night, and you know that as well as I do."

"Don't get upset with me. I just called to tell you what I heard. I don't make the decisions. Luke Powell does, and I didn't get this from him."

"And you won't. Our man's right here under our noses and flaunting it."

"If he's here, we'll find him."

"Good. Keep me posted."

"Are you sure you don't want to change places? That house you're in looks like a palace compared to this motel room. Of course, you are having to play bodyguard to a woman who looks as if she might deliver at any second. How's it going?"

"Not bad. Now I need to get off this phone and do my job. But informant or no informant, the attack last night was the work of Joshua Caraway. You can make book on it."

"It seemed a little bloodless for a Caraway job. For that matter, so did the explosion at the Brewsters'."

"He used what was on hand."

"And if he's here, we'll find him. If he's in St. Louis, your pregnant lady may have an enemy of her own."

Bart headed back to the balcony, but he'd lost his taste for surf and sand. Megan was still standing by the railing, the wind lifting her hair from her neck and tossing it about. Head high, shoulders straight, she looked regal. Most definitely pregnant, but still attractive.

Classic was the word that came to mind. High cheekbones darkened by the sun, full, sensual lips. And Joshua Caraway's latest target, regardless of the St. Louis rumor. Even that was probably of Joshua's doing. The man was a heartless scumbag with a penchant for murder.

He swallowed the anger that balled in his throat. "Sorry about the interruption."

"Was it good news?"

"Not unless you believe no news is good news. Are you hungry?"

"I could eat."

"Then let's go find one of those cozy restaurants we talked about with a table in the back corner so I can gaze into your eyes."

"Does the FBI give out Oscars for best performance by an agent?"

"Yeah, my shelves are full of them. Come over one night and I'll let you hold one."

"You are too kind."

"Do we just leave Leroy here alone to finish his job?"

"Sure. It won't be the first time. His mom is in charge of the place when I'm away, and he does work for me when I'm in New Orleans."

"Just how many people have a key to this place?"

"Apparently half the town, but don't worry. It's a small town. We trust one another."

Add one more stop to their afternoon's excursion—a hardware store to pick up new locks.

"MY BROTHER-IN-LAW FORGOT to mention that the seafood in this area was fantastic."

Megan's interest piqued when she thought he was talking about his family then dropped as she realized this was his pretend brother-in-law who'd had a pretend wedding in Mobile. She wondered if anyone ever got to really know the man behind the facade.

She took another bite of her shrimp salad without bothering to comment. They'd decided on the Oyster House for lunch. It wasn't particularly quiet or cozy, but the food was great and it was in the town of Gulf Shores, which was on the way to Dr. Brown's office.

"So what do female executives do for fun in New Orleans?" he asked, trying once again to drew her into conversation.

She toyed with the handle of her fork. "Sex, drugs and rock and roll. What else?"

"Now you're putting me on."

"Don't I look like a fun lady to you?"

"Fun, but reserved. Probably assertive and demanding at work, but more laid-back when you're on your own time."

"You're intuitive as well as a good actor."

"I'm a man of many talents."

"I'll just bet. But to answer your question, when I'm home on weekends, I enjoy inline skating at Audubon Park, shopping, going to local festivals, of which we have at least a half-dozen happening somewhere in and around the city almost every weekend. I attend plays, concerts—all kinds of music—and I never miss a Saints game if I'm in town when they're playing at home."

"I could use a few weekends like that."

"Come to New Orleans. We have it all."

"I've been there once, for Mardi Gras. I had a blast."

"I probably don't even want to know what you did that trip."

"Good, because I'd never own up."

"We're not that decadent all the time, and the French Quarter is only a small part of the city. I live in the downtown area in what's known as the Arts District. There are galleries, coffeehouses and restaurants practically right outside my door."

"You travel the world and own a condominium in downtown New Orleans and a gigantic beach house in paradise. A nice life, if you can get it."

"It's not as glamorous as it sounds. Mostly I work. That's why I love coming to Pelican's Roost. It's the one place where I can get away from it all. Unfortunately, it hasn't worked that way this time."

"But you have a new lover in your life," he teased, going all out to keep lunch on a light note. She had to admire him for that. She was certain from his reactions that the phone call back at the house had been bad news.

Bart forked the soft-shell crab that came on his seafood platter. "Are you sure I'm supposed to eat this."

"I don't know. Give me a bite of it and I'll tell you if it's fit to eat."

He broke off one of the legs with his fork and fed it to her. She chewed and swallowed. "Mmm. Perfect."

"I didn't think you'd actually eat it."

"Are you kidding? Soft-shell crab's a delicacy. Haven't you ever tried it?"

"No, and you have to admit, it's a weird-looking creature. You Southern girls will eat anything."

"No way. That's just a Northern boy's fantasy."

They both laughed, and the sound of it surprised Megan. She couldn't remember when she'd laughed last, but she had the feeling it was before she'd made the decision to go through the procedures for becoming a surrogate mother to Jackie's baby.

Bart tried the crab. He swallowed and smacked his lips appreciatively. "That is good. If we keep eating like this, I may never want to go home."

"And where would home be?"

He winked conspiratorially. "A world away from the warm southern shores of Alabama."

He finished his crab while she munched on her salad and looked around the restaurant. It was fairly busy, but she didn't see anyone she recognized. She wasn't surprised. The number of permanent residents along the beach had grown steadily in recent years, and even in December there were some tourists.

When Bart finished the last French fry, he pushed his empty plate to the side and stretched his hands across the table. "Are you ready to look into my eyes seductively?"

"It would be a waste of time. I don't know a soul in the place."

"We can practice."

She moistened her lips with her tongue, slowly, sensually, and then leaned into the table—as much as she could with her protruding stomach—and gave him a coquettish smile.

He took her hands in his. "Forget the practice. You have that part down pat. A man would never have a chance against your wiles."

"You've seen mine. Now show me yours."

"I've never refused a lady that." He squeezed her hands and stared deep into her eyes. Determined not to blink, she stared back at him until the waitress came to refill their water glasses, then burst into giggles.

"You giggle like a schoolgirl," he said as the waitress walked away smiling.

"I do *not* giggle."

"You *did*."

"Well, I don't make a habit of it." She slipped her hands from his and leaned back in her chair.

"Don't get so uptight. I wasn't complaining. Just stating the truth. I like the way you laugh."

It amazed her how quickly he picked up on her moods and read her reactions. It had to be the result of his training. No man she'd ever met had developed the talent. "I like the way I laugh, too," she admitted. "I just don't do it often enough."

"So why now?"

"I don't know. Maybe having a killer on my trail does something strange to my inhibitions or maybe it's just knowing how close I came last night to never laughing again."

"That's not as bizarre as it sounds. Danger affects people in different ways. In some it brings out the best and they become stronger and more resilient than they knew they could be. Others completely fall apart.''

''That's a strange bit of information to have at your fingertips. Don't you ever grow weary of dealing with murderers and criminals day after day?''

''All the time, but I can't see myself doing any other kind of work. How about you?''

''I love my job. There's never a dull moment—hectic and exhausting, but never dull.''

''Don't you get tired of the travel?''

''Occasionally. Not often. I was a bookworm growing up, and now I get to go to the places I read and dreamed about back then.''

He touched his fingertips to her cheek. ''I can't quite see you as a bookworm. You seem too enthused with life to be satisfied with mere words.''

''I didn't have a lot of choice. My mother was a dancer, and we moved from town to town, from show to show. We never stayed in one place long enough for me to make a lot of friends, but as long as I had a book, I wasn't lonely.''

''Weren't you?''

He'd done it again. Seen right through her facade. She shook her head. ''Do you tell fortunes, or just read minds?''

''Neither. You're lousy at lying.''

''A woman can't be perfect at everything.''

''It must have been an unusual life, growing up with a dancer.''

''Not only a dancer, but a former Miss Alabama. Even now she's striking. Bigger than life.''

''Did the two of you get along?''

''We never argued back then, but I was always aware that I put a damper on her lifestyle.''

"Then why did she have a child?"

"She didn't mean to. I was a mistake, the result of a brief affair with a man who ran out on her the minute he found out she was pregnant. That's why I'm a Lancaster."

"Have you ever wondered about your father or tried to find him?"

"Not lately. I have enough problems dealing with my mother. I'm not about to go searching for an additional parent. Besides, he was no more than a sperm donor. He doesn't know me and never wanted to. As far as I'm concerned, I had no father. Why the sudden interest in my family?"

"I'm just curious."

She doubted that. He was on a case. This was a job to him. *She* was a job to him, and she needed to keep that in mind before she went spilling her guts to a man who only existed in the FBI case files.

She looked up as an extremely attractive man walked in alone. He wore jeans and a plain cotton shirt open at the neck. His gaze scanned the room, then stopped on her. Apprehension skittered crazily along her nerve endings as he followed the waitress to a spot just a few tables down from where they were sitting. "Did you see that man?"

"I saw him. What about him?"

"I've never seen him around here before, and something about him made me uneasy."

"Don't worry about him."

But she was worried. She was certain he'd focused on her when he'd walked in, and then deliberately avoided looking at her when he'd walked past. "That could be the man who tried to kill me, Bart. Watch him and see if he looks this way."

"It's not him."

"You don't know that. You said you didn't get a good

look at him the other night. Get a good look now and let's get out of here.'' She was overreacting, but she couldn't help it. She could all but feel his hands on her head, pushing her under the water.

"Relax, Megan. The guy's all right."

"You don't know, and don't use that patronizing FBI tone on me."

He leaned in close and kept his voice low. "I'm sorry for the tone, but I do know. He's one of us."

"Another agent?"

He nodded. "Now, you're officially in on private information. Just don't do anything to give him away."

"How many others are in town?"

"There are three of us in all."

Tiny alarms sounded in her head. Three FBI agents all here to protect her and her unborn child. It didn't take a genius to realize that something was wrong with that picture. "There's more to this story than you've told me, isn't there? This isn't about protecting me and my baby at all." Her voice was rising, but she didn't care. She was being used, and she wanted all the facts and she wanted them now.

He pushed his plate away. "This isn't the place to talk, Megan. Let me pay the bill and we'll get out of here."

"Then we'll talk in the car, because if you don't have a very good reason for lying to me, for keeping me here to play hide-and-seek with a killer, I'm on my way back to New Orleans. And you can take the bureau policy, your fake ID and your imitation concern for me and the baby and drop them off the face of the earth."

BART PULLED Megan into the car. The restaurant was too crowded to risk having Megan cause a scene. This was his fault. He let down his guard for one minute, broke one rule, and things flew apart like an exploding firecracker inside a paper bag.

Megan was supposed to be on a strict need-to-know basis as far as information pertaining to the crime was concerned. He shouldn't have told her that the man in the Oyster House was an agent, should have realized she was too smart not to put two and two together.

He stared out the front window at the endless water, at the glorious bands of blues and greens, and suddenly the car seemed cramped, the air thick. "Do you feel like walking?"

"As long as you're talking."

He opened his car door. She opened her own before he had time to circle the car and do it for her. He tried to take her arm as they took the path to the beach, but she jerked away. He had no idea what was going on in her mind other than the fact that she knew he hadn't been totally honest with her.

Even now he'd have to watch how much he gave away, but he had a hard time lying to Megan. It wasn't just the pregnancy. It was the woman herself that was getting to him. Her honesty. Her directness. The way her eyes sparked and darted and revealed her emotions. They reached the beach and Megan stepped out of her sandals. He bent and picked them up.

"Thanks."

"You're welcome."

"I'll carry them," she said, her voice hard with anger. "You can stop playing Mr. Helpful. No more breakfasts in bed, opening car doors or carrying my shoes. I've had enough of the pretenses of Bart Cromwell, enough of being your job."

"Cooking your breakfast was not in my job description. I did it because I wanted to. Same goes for your shoes."

Still he handed her the sandals. "What do you want to know, Megan? I'll be as honest as I can."

"As honest as you can. It's my life and the life of my baby we're talking about, but you'll be as honest as you can. Doesn't that sound pompous and bureaucratic even to you?"

He exhaled sharply, releasing a stream of frustration. "I'm taking care of business. That's all." A thankless, dangerous, sometimes disgusting job tracking down murderous bastards, and days like this he wondered why he bothered.

No. He knew why he bothered. It was for Megan and the baby and thousands of other innocent people who became victims of a criminal element that grew larger and more vicious all the time.

"I want to know why Ben and Jackie were killed. And don't give me that hogwash about how there were some indications that it was not an accident. You know more than that. If you didn't, there wouldn't be three agents down here searching for the man behind this. You wouldn't be using me as bait to catch him."

"You're not bait. You're a target. There's a difference." No matter that the line between the two was exceedingly thin in this case. "And Ben Brewster is not the man's real name."

"Here we go again. Another fake. I suppose he was with the FBI, too."

"No. He was taken into the witness protection program eight years ago when he testified against a hit man named Joshua Caraway, known better by his earned nickname, The Butcher. Ben was part of the mob himself, but he ratted and asked for protection when he saw Joshua kill one man and his whole family. The victim was an FBI agent."

"Did you know him?"

"Very well. Him and his family."

"I'm sorry. I'm really sorry, but I have to know everything. I can't go on walking around in a blur of half truths."

"I'm trying, Megan. Just hang in here with me."

"Did Jackie know that Ben had been in the witness protection program?"

"Not unless Ben told her. He'd skipped out of the program a few years earlier."

"Why would he do that?"

"People do it all the time. My guess is he was tired of the restrictions and rules and felt it had been long enough and that no one would be looking for him anymore."

"Obviously he was wrong."

"He never expected Joshua Caraway to be on the loose again."

"Why would a brutal murderer be released from prison in eight years?"

"He wasn't released. He escaped. Six weeks ago, he apparently rode out of the prison walls inside a news van that was there doing a story on the plight of prisoners in for life."

"Got out of prison and tracked down Ben." Images erupted in her mind, the way they always did when she thought of Jackie being trapped in that explosion. Jackie and a husband who was really someone else.

"He'd vowed to get Ben on the day he was sentenced, promised him he'd come back and kill him and every member of his family in the same horrible fashion Ben had witnessed."

She stopped and stared out at the water, one hand over her eyes to block the sun. "So you followed me," she said, "watched every move I made, waiting for your chance to capture Joshua Caraway. Didn't you even once think I had the right to know all of this? I might have taken precautions to protect myself. I could have moved out of the country or hired my own bodyguard.''

"We couldn't be positive he'd come after you. We weren't certain until the other night that he even knew about the baby. Until he tried to kill you, we were only playing a hunch."

"How would he have found out about the baby?" She asked stepping over a large, broken shell.

"The same way I did. By talking to the neighbors after the explosion."

"That would be risky, wouldn't it?"

"He's the kind of man who'd enjoy seeing the horror he'd created." He explained, dreading that he had nothing but chilling details to share. "And there's more."

"Somehow I knew there would be."

"Jackie's neighbor didn't know your name. All she knew was that the surrogate parent was a dear friend who had come from the same town as Jackie. I had to use my FBI privileges to get your name from Jackie's doctor."

"Then how would this Joshua Caraway know who I am?" she insisted.

"Jackie's doctor's office was broken into. Nothing was taken except for drugs, but whoever broke in could have looked at Jackie's records."

"And her medical records would contain my name as the recipient of the fertilized egg."

"Exactly."

Megan eased down to a sitting position on the sand and hugged her skirt and her arms around her knees. "Eight years in prison and the man walked out only to kill again. It's hard to imagine what goes on in the mind of a person like that."

"Revenge can be a powerful motivator."

"Then why doesn't it affect all of us? Suppose I had gone through life trying to exact some type of revenge against a man who'd wanted no part of me or my mother. Suppose I spent my days and nights now angered that my mother pursued her own happiness with little thought for mine. I'm aware of those things. I'm sure they even affect my personality and my relationships, but I don't let them eat away at me until they destroy my humanity."

"That's the difference between most of us and a man like Joshua Caraway," he answered. "I can't explain it. No one has, though there are countless theories on the subject."

He sat down beside her. He longed to put an arm around her shoulder, to pull her close, to comfort her. But even if she let him, it would be a mistake. He'd already let her get to him, made him feel things and think thoughts that had no place in a situation where one mistake could cost her her life.

"Does Ben have other family?" She asked, her voice still strained.

"A mother. She's being tailed as well. There have been no attempts on her life."

"Susan. That was the neighbor who told you about the baby, wasn't it? She and Jackie were close. She was there when Jackie endured the three miscarriages, and when the doctor told her that with her diabetes it would be dangerous for her to try again."

"It was Susan," he admitted, "and that's pretty much what she told me. That the explosion was doubly tragic considering the fact that Jackie was about to finally get the daughter she'd been praying for."

"Did you tell Susan you were from the FBI?"

"No. She thought I was a reporter, but she did say that she had given the same information to someone else."

"I still wake up at night and imagine Jackie's body being blown to bits. How could he do that to Jackie and Ben. How could he?"

Megan closed her eyes, and he watched the tears squeeze past her lids and slide down her cheek. He couldn't stand to sit by and do nothing. He pulled her into his arms and held her close while sobs shook her body.

It was long minutes later before she pulled away and rubbed her eyes with the heels of her hands. "I don't know why I did that. I didn't even cry like that at the funeral."

"Cry all you want. Tears cleanse the soul. At least that's what my mother says."

"Would that be your real mother or the one created for the current performance?"

"That would be my real mother. She's a great lady. You'd like her and she'd love you."

Megan sniffed and took a wadded tissue form her pocket and wiped her nose. "She's fond of crybabies, is she?"

Her lips curled in the slightest of smiles, but he was glad to see it. "Are you ready to go?"

"One more question," she said finally looking at him. "When was the break-in at the doctor's office?"

"December third."

"One day before I left New Orleans and drove to Orange Beach. You were on the scene quickly."

"If I hadn't been, you'd be dead."

"But I'm the bait, aren't I?" she insisted. Joshua Caraway's probably moved to the top of your infamous Most Wanted list and I'm the lure who can reel him in. This isn't about me and my baby so much as it's about Joshua Caraway.''

''That's part of it, but I'd never intended on sacrificing you. If I had, I could have gone after him the other night and let you drown.''

''That was probably instinct kicking in.''

''You're too smart for your own good.'' He tucked a thumb under her chin and tilted her face toward his. ''But for the record, I'm not sorry I saved you, and even if Joshua Caraway is never caught, I still won't be sorry.''

Her gaze met his. Her eyes were filled with doubt, fear, grief, a medley of emotions she should never have had to feel. He hoped his were not as transparent. He stood and pulled her to her feet.

She brushed the sand from her skirt and smoothed her hair with the palms of her hands. ''I wish you'd told me the truth from the beginning.''

''I'm going against rules to even tell you now. We have no proof that Joshua Caraway is behind any of this. It's just gut instinct that made me think the explosion was his doing. But the break-in at the doctor's office and the subsequent attack on you gives my theory a lot more credence.''

''Okay, Bart Cromwell, or whoever you are. He not only killed your friend, he killed mine, too, so fasten me to the end of the pole and cast me out there. We've got a murderer to catch.''

December 13

MEGAN WANDERED through the rooms of Pelican's Roost. It had been five days since the attempt on her life, five days of wondering how and when Joshua Caraway would strike again. Bart was certain that he would, and that knowledge cast a shroud of fear that vacillated between suffocating oppression to a random uneasiness that churned inside her like the choppy waters of the Gulf.

He was out there somewhere, waiting for the right time, the right opportunity. A quick hit that would kill Ben Brewster's child and her in the process. A baby who had no parents. All she had was Megan. But there were people out there who'd love her as their own. All Megan had to do was call the adoption agency and they'd put the wheels in motion.

Only she couldn't bring herself to make the call. "I never thought I'd feel so close to you, sweetie. You're so much a part of me now. We breathe the same air and eat the same food. And I love feeling you move and tumble in there." She rubbed her stomach and felt a tremble of excitement knowing the time for the baby to be born was so near.

The visit to the doctor's office had gone well. Her weight was in line, the baby's heartbeat was strong and he thought the baby might even come a couple of days early. Best of all, he'd assured her that her records were confidential. He'd tell no one the identity of the parents of the baby she was carrying.

She walked the hall on the third floor, stopping in each room, trying to focus on the good memories she'd always associated with the beach house, hoping they could work some kind of magic on her rattled nerves. Every summer and every Christmas her mother would pack her bags and send her to Grandma's house. It was a way of getting rid of her, but Megan had been as excited about going as her mother had been about getting her out of her hair.

She and her grandmother had taken long walks, combing the beaches for shells, and then they'd come home and have breakfast in the sun-drenched nook overlooking the Gulf. In the summer, she'd swim out as far as she could on a huge rubber float and then ride the waves back into shore. At Christmas, they'd always put up a huge tree in the family room and decorate it with seashells they painted themselves.

A tree might be just what she needed now. Some sign of normalcy in a world where there was none.

She went searching for Bart and found him in the bedroom he'd claimed as his, sitting at the desk and typing on a laptop computer. She stood for a moment watching him before he turned and saw her. The second he did, he switched frames, obviously not wanting her to see what he was doing.

"I didn't hear you come in."

"You were too engrossed in what you were doing."

"Spinning my wheels. But I'm open to doing something more entertaining. Any ideas?"

"Actually, I was thinking I'd like to go shopping for a Christmas tree."

"That's a great idea." He jumped up from the computer. "How does the song go? We need a little Christmas. We should buy some popcorn, too. And a CD. We always ate popcorn and listened to Christmas music when we decorated our tree." He fished in his pockets and pulled out his keys. "We can take my car and tie the tree to the top. Can I get your coat for you?"

"I have a jacket in the downstairs closet. I'll get it on the way out."

"Then we're off."

The man never ceased to amaze her. If anyone had told her five days ago that she'd adjust this quickly to living with a man, she'd have thought they were crazy. But then, she'd never been around a man quite like Bart Cromwell.

He fit with the beach, so well that she'd accused him of being a beach bum in his real life. All she had to do was mention she was ready for a walk and he jumped at the chance to play in the surf, even got in some swimming on days the temperature climbed into the seventies, though he never let her out of his sight. And while he didn't build sand castles, he had sculpted an extremely realistic turtle out of damp sand.

By the time she retrieved her jacket, he was waiting at the front door. Unfortunately, the phone rang, and these days it was never good news. She picked up the receiver.

"Hello."

"Darling. I'm so glad I caught you. It's been positively ages."

Her heart plunged to her stomach. There was only one explanation for the call. Her mother had found out about the baby.

Chapter Seven

Megan listened to her mother make small talk, knowing that was not why she'd called. She leaned against the desk where Bart had been working at his laptop. "How did you know I was here?"

"John told me."

Ah, good old John. "Did you call for something specific?"

"Can't a mother call her daughter just to talk?"

Most moms could and did, but Marilyn was not most moms. Megan waited through the awkward silence that followed, knowing her mother was about to tell her why she'd really called.

"Actually, darling, I didn't call John. He called me. He's quite worried about you."

Megan rubbed her left temple, fighting off the beginning of what would probably turn into a giant headache. "Exactly what did John tell you?"

"Everything that you should have told me months ago, that you are carrying your friend Jackie's baby and that she and her husband were killed in a tragic accident."

"Then he caught you up on all the news."

"I can't believe I had to hear it from him. My own

daughter, pregnant, and I didn't even know it. Of course, it's not like the baby's yours.''

"No, it's not like it's mine. I guess that's why I didn't bother calling you.''

"Are you totally huge?''

She looked down at her stomach. "I'd say huge pretty much covers it.''

"Don't worry. A few months of dieting and a rigorous exercise routine, and you'll get your figure back. It's just a shame you're going to have those ugly stretch marks for a child that's not even yours.''

Megan drummed her fingers on the desk. If her mother said "not even yours" one more time, she might be forced to hurl the telephone across the room. "What else did John say when he called you?''

"Oh, the poor man. He's so worried about you. He's afraid you're about to make a big mistake, darling.''

"It's too late to change my mind about having the baby. She's due December twenty-seventh.''

"A girl?''

"That's what it looked like in the sonogram.''

"This reminds me of when you were born. You were all red and cute, and the tiniest thing. I was afraid to hold you at first.''

Megan tried to imagine her mother caring for a helpless infant, but the image refused to gel. The memories she had of her already were too ingrained. Beautiful. Dancing. Dieting. "I don't think this baby will be that little," she said, pulling herself back to the conversation. "At least not judging by the way I look.''

"I'm sure you'll get your shape back eventually. But I didn't call to talk about the pregnancy. I'm concerned about what you're going to do once the baby is born.''

"Diet and exercise rigorously, I suppose, just like you said."

"I mean what you're going to do about the baby." Her exasperation was evident from her tone. "John fears that you might be thinking about keeping it instead of giving it up for adoption."

"John *fears* I might keep the baby." Aggravation swelled inside her. "I really don't know why John would concern himself at all with my personal life."

"The reason is obvious. He's still in love with you. You broke his heart when you called off the wedding at the last minute. Ansel and I already had our airline reservations."

Some broken heart. John had been involved with another woman in a matter of weeks. Which was fine by her. She hadn't wanted him to suffer. When push came to shove, she simply wasn't ready to make a commitment. "John is not in love with me, Mother. More likely, he's worried that I'll leave him in the lurch with the project we're working on."

"It's not John I'm concerned about anyway. It's you. I know how upset you must be over Jackie's death, but surely she wouldn't expect you to give up your freedom and your lifestyle to take care of a baby—"

"Who's not even mine." This time they said it in unison. "Millions of women raise children, Mother. Some of them even enjoy it. But you don't need to worry. I have no plans to keep the baby."

No plans at all. She'd just give birth and then hand the newborn over to someone else to love. Another woman would rock her to sleep and feed her and hold her close when she cried. "I have to go, Mother."

"Do you need me to be there when the baby is born? Ansel has a trip planned for my birthday and we have guests coming in for the holidays, but if you need me, I'll just walk out on my responsibilities and come running.''

"No. I'm doing fine. A friend is staying with me. You just stay home and enjoy the holidays with Ansel and your friends.''

"Okay, but I'm here for you, darling. If you need anything, you call. And I'm glad you're not thinking of saddling yourself with a baby. This is the prime of your life.''

"I'm twelve years older than you were when you had me, Mother. My prime is fading fast.''

It wasn't responsibility she was afraid of. It was knowing she could never give Jackie's baby the kind of love and care it needed. She was a career woman. Driven. Focused. Competent. It was the only life she was sure she could handle. But she would have a word with John Hardison. He had overstepped his bounds and she wouldn't tolerate his interference in her personal life.

When she hung up the phone, she realized Bart was staring at her.

"I take it that was not a pleasant conversation.''

"It was typical of conversations I have with my mother.''

"Is that why you're holding to the edge of that desk so hard that your knuckles are turning white?''

"No.'' She flexed her hands and moved away from the desk. "I learned long ago to accept her the way she is.''

"So what teed you off?''

"Dear John Hardison. The only time he ever met my mother was at my grandmother's funeral, yet he took the liberty to call her to discuss my having this baby.''

"Do you want to talk about it?''

"When I calm down, but I'll do my talking with John. I believe in tackling problems at their source.''

"And I believe it's a good time to buy a Christmas

tree.'' He started a rousing chorus of ''Jingle Bells'' as they walked down the steps arm in arm.

A killer, John, her mother, her nerves stretched to their limits. She had plenty of reasons to sink into despair. But it was hard to be miserable when a gorgeous man was singing ''Jingle Bells…'' to her.

FENELDA STOOD at the sink rinsing the potatoes she'd just peeled and cubed for tonight's dinner. Her son, Leroy, was a few feet away, yanking the tab from a can of beer he'd just taken from the refrigerator. He drank too much, but if that was all he was doing, she could live with it.

It was the drugs that worried her most. Once he started on them, he couldn't stop, and she couldn't afford another stay at the hospital. The next time, he'd have to take whatever punishment the judge meted out, even if it meant jail.

''Did you fix the leaky faucet at the Lancaster place today?''

''Yep.''

''Was Megan home?''

''Not when I got there, but she came in a few minutes later. It was a good thing. She took the key from under the steps. Guess she's not as trusting as her grandmother was, or maybe her boyfriend's not.''

''She didn't bring a boyfriend with her.''

''Then I reckon she found one after she got here. Some guy was with her, and he's staying there, too.''

''How do you know?''

''He didn't try to keep it a secret. Besides, I looked around. His clothes are in one of the closets. They're not in her bedroom, but that doesn't mean they're not sleeping together.''

''Don't go around town talking that trash. Megan's not

that kind of woman. Whoever the man is, I'm sure he's just a friend.''

"Yeah, sure, Mama. I guess her mother was a virtuous lady, too. That's how she ended up with Megan.''

"You don't know what you're talking about.''

"I know more than you think.'' He turned the beer up and guzzled it down. "Don't bother cooking for me. I'm going out tonight.''

"Don't do anything to get in trouble, Leroy. No drugs. You promised.''

"I couldn't buy any if I wanted them. I'm broke.'' He pulled his wallet out of his back pocket and spread it open. All she saw were a few ones, though she'd paid him for helping her clean her regular houses last week. Not that he'd earned it. She had to keep on him every second to get him to finish even the simplest of tasks.

"I wish you were more like Mark Cox. He calls me up looking for work to do. And when he has a job to do, he does it right. I can recommend him to anyone without worrying.''

"You want me to be like Mark Cox? That's rich, Mama. Really rich. Why not wish I was like a movie star or a basketball player, someone with some real cash to blow.''

She heard the front door slam a few minutes later. He'd be out late as usual. She'd be up worrying. He might be broke now, but he'd managed to get money for drugs before when she thought he hadn't had a dime on him.

She didn't like to think he'd stoop to stealing, but to be on the safe side, she wouldn't send him to any of the houses she took care of again unless she was with him.

It was a sad day when a mother couldn't trust her own son. She was almost glad her husband wasn't here to see this, God rest his soul.

MEGAN STOOD BACK and eyed the tree from top to bottom. "It's crooked."

Bart put down the string of lights he'd just removed from the package. "Looks perfectly straight."

"No. It's tipping to the right just a little."

He walked over and stood beside her. "What are you, an official Christmas-tree critic?"

"I hate for things to be crooked. It makes me want to straighten them every time I pass."

"Wouldn't bother me a bit, as long as it wasn't falling over." But he crawled back under it and fiddled with the trunk and the stand.

His behind stuck up in the air and she found herself staring at the pull of his jeans across his firm buttocks. She was pregnant, but she wasn't beyond being titillated by the sight. Bart Cromwell was a very sexy man.

"Tell me when it's straight."

"Just a teensy-weensy bit more to the left. Keep going—that's it. Perfect."

"That's the way I like to hear a woman talk." He crawled out from under the tree and ran his fingers through his mussed hair. "I'll string the lights if you'll pop the popcorn and make the hot cocoa," he said.

"Popcorn will spoil your dinner."

"Not mine. Besides, we can have a late dinner. I'll cook."

"You mean open the soup can all by yourself?"

"You are heartless."

She went to the kitchen and stuck a package into the microwave and set the controls for four minutes. Bending, she pulled a boiler from the bottom cabinet. Bending was difficult, but straightening up again was the real challenge. "You do make maneuvering around the kitchen a challenge, little one."

While the milk was heating, she mixed the cocoa, sugar, vanilla and a spoonful of milk into a smooth paste and thought again of her mother's phone call. John and her mother. Funny, she'd never thought of their being alike before, yet listening to her mother talk tonight, her thoughts on keeping the baby had sounded much like John's. And she'd come within days of marrying him.

She pushed the disturbing thoughts aside. She wanted one night of reprieve, an hour or two to decorate a Christmas tree without the emotional hassles that went with relationships and killers and motherless babies.

She stared out the window. The sun was setting, painting the undersides of the clouds in brilliant shades of yellow and orange. Bing Crosby's rendition of ''White Christmas'' filled the house with music and memories. The smells of popcorn and chocolate and the pungent odor of fresh-cut spruce touched every breath. And a hunk of an FBI agent who called himself Bart Cromwell was stringing lights on a Christmas tree in her living room.

The whole scenario seemed somewhat surreal, but she was going to make a concerted effort to enjoy it for at least as long as it took to decorate the tree.

IF HIS FRIENDS could see him now, they'd be absolutely green with envy, Bart decided as he circled the tree, tucking the lights into the branches. Decorating a Christmas tree in a rambling old beach house with the Gulf of Mexico for a backdrop. Add to that the company of a woman who was not only beautiful and intelligent, but had a warmth about her that made him think of cuddling beneath a blanket and letting nature take its course.

This John fellow had to be kicking himself all over New Orleans for letting her get away. Women like Megan Lancaster didn't just waltz into a man's life every day.

Not that he was an expert on women. He'd never had a clue what they wanted from a man, as evidenced by his own blown marriage.

He looked up as Megan walked in. "Now, this is what I call living. A beautiful woman bearing food. Don't let my supervisor hear about this. He'll want to cut my pay."

"I'll never tell—unless, of course, you quit before the tree is fully decorated."

"I've done the hard part already." He toed the empty light cartons out of the way and plugged the cord into the floor socket. A hundred sparkling white lights lit the room with a magical glow. "What do you think? Does it pass the inspection of the tree critic?"

"It's beautiful."

"You mean not one light needs to be rearranged."

"I wouldn't go that far." She looked down and patted her stomach. "What's that you say, little one? You want to pop out and have a look? Good, you do that before Christmas and you can be here for all the fun. Just don't pop out tonight."

He took his cocoa, but his eyes were on Megan. He didn't know what had prompted the phone call from her mother, but from the little he'd overheard, he suspected it had to do with whether or not Megan was going to keep the baby and raise it as her own since her friend was no longer around to take care of it.

He'd heard Megan say she had no intention of keeping the baby, but he had doubts about that. A woman who went around talking and singing to an unborn child was not likely to want to shove it out of her life the second it was born.

All of which was none of his business. His job was to keep her alive.

"What was your best Christmas present ever?" she

asked. hanging a shiny red ornament on the end of a branch.

"I'll have to think about that," he said. "I guess it would have to be the bike I got when I was six. I was so excited, I rode it in the snow. What about you?"

"A baby doll when I was four. She's still here somewhere, most likely packed away in one of the boxes in the cupola. I used to beg my mother for a little sister, but the doll was as close as I got."

Bart joined in the decorating, hanging ornaments on the high branches so Megan wouldn't have to stretch to reach them. "What was the best gift you ever gave someone?"

"Moneywise or just the one I was most excited about giving?"

"The one you got a kick out of," he said.

"That's a hard one." She grabbed another bite of popcorn and another ornament to hang. "I guess that would have to be my first year in college. I painted a picture of Pelican's Roost and wrote a poem about how much my grandmother had meant in my life. I gave them both to her for Christmas. She cried when she read the poem, said it was the best present she'd ever received. Actually, we both cried. The picture's hanging in the hall."

"You painted that? I'm impressed. I thought it was done by a professional."

"That's why I insisted she hang it in the hall and not over the fireplace where she wanted it. My amateur status shows up more in bright light. What about you? Best present you ever gave someone."

"Mine's going to sound silly compared to yours."

"Come on. You have to tell. It's your turn."

"Then I guess it would have to be the dollhouse I made my little sister. My dad helped me with the sawing and let me use his tools to do it, but I did most of the work.

Mom got some carpet samples for me to put on the floors and some wallpaper samples. It was really neat, if I do say so myself.''

''How old were you?''

''Twelve. It was my woodworking project for Scouts, and I took a lot of ribbing from the guys but it was worth it. She was thrilled. My mom swears she played with it up until she went on her first date.''

''Is she a lot younger than you?''

''Six years, but I have two brothers in between.''

''Wait a minute.'' She stepped back from the tree, ornament in hand. ''Is this Bart Cromwell's family or the family that belongs to the real you?''

Damn. The real him, and it had all just slipped out, as if he were on a date instead of on the job. He had to get hold of the situation fast. But he wasn't going to lie to her. ''It's the real me.''

She smiled and her whole face seemed to light up, putting the sparkling tree to shame.

''It must have been fun growing up in a large family.''

''Most of the time. We fussed a lot, typical sibling stuff, but we're all close now. It's wilder than a pack of screaming hyenas when we all get together, which we do every Fourth of July and every New Year's.''

''But not Christmas?''

''No, I usually go home for the big day if I'm not on assignment, but the rest of them don't. They all have families and in-laws, and one of my brothers is a pediatrician, so he's on call sometimes. So we just have Christmas again on New Years Eve.''

''Does your mother like having you all home at once?''

''Are you kidding? She lives for it. She's even worse now that there are six grandchildren. Once they all start opening presents, the house resembles the North Pole after being attacked by a pack of deranged elves.''

"Lucky grandchildren. All that love and laughter."

She grew quiet for a moment then threw herself into the chorus of "Rudolph the Red-Nosed Reindeer." He sang along with her, and they worked that way until the tree was finished.

A stranger might mistake the scene for one of serenity. But a stranger wouldn't know the tension that crackled between a couple when the man was so attracted to the woman it was all he could do not to give his feelings away. When the man was only there to protect the beautiful pregnant woman from a killer.

"Are you ready for me to hang the angel on top of the tree?" he asked.

His hand brushed hers as he took the angel from her, and he felt a rush of desire so strong it almost took his breath away. He stepped away, still shaken and determined not to let her see how the incidental touch had affected him.

This was crazy. He never fell for the woman he was protecting. It was stupid and dangerous. If he kept it up, he'd have to remove himself from the case, get one of the other agents to replace him.

Only he knew he'd never be able to do that. As long as Joshua Caraway was on the loose, he'd be right here, making sure The Butcher didn't get to Megan the way he had to Jackie and Ben Brewster.

He placed the fragile doll of white lace and silvery wire on top of the tree making sure she was perfectly straight. When he was finished, he stepped back to admire his handiwork.

Megan walked over, took his arm and looked up at him

with her big, dark eyes. "Not half-bad," she whispered. "We make a pretty good team."

He swallowed hard, knowing she wouldn't be saying that if she had any idea what he'd felt a minute ago. And even now, he was far too aware of her nearness.

"It's too late for the sunset, but we can still take a walk on the beach. There's going to be a full moon tonight."

A moonlit walk on the beach the way he was feeling right now would be like flashing food in front of a starving man, then telling him all he could do was smell it.

"I don't think that's a good idea."

"I guess it would be a little risky walking after dark with a murderer on the loose."

"Yeah. I'm going to grab a shower, unless you have another decorating chore for me."

"Go ahead. I'll just sit here and admire the tree for a few minutes longer."

"I think you should call Penny and tell her we'll come to her party."

"We don't have to do that."

"I think it's a good idea, for several reasons."

"What reasons are those?"

"Christmas is good for you. I've never seen you as relaxed as you've been tonight. And I think we may need to be a little more convincing that I'm a lover and not here in another capacity."

"So that we can pull Joshua Caraway out from his hiding place?"

"If he thinks we're in Orange Beach looking for him, he's going to keep a lower profile than if he feels free to move around town. We can't arrest him if we can't find him."

"Then let's go the party, lover boy."

"Better watch it. I get really turned on when a woman talks dirty to me."

And in this case, he was already there. He walked away from the sparkling lights of the tree and from feelings he had to tamp down so far they'd never see daylight. A cold shower should go a long way toward doing that. And if that wasn't enough, he could throw in a few bloody images from the files of Joshua Caraway.

MEGAN CLIMBED THE STAIRS slowly, dealing with the myriad conflicting thoughts that fought for position in her mind. Decorating the tree with Bart had provided a couple of hours of relief, but nothing could wipe away the pain and the fear that constantly tiptoed around the edges of her very existence.

Not fear for herself, but for the baby that a man known as The Butcher was determined to destroy. Only he hadn't butchered Jackie and Ben. He'd caused an explosion to rip through their house and blow them into shreds of charred flesh. Her stomach turned inside out and she grabbed the railing for support.

He hadn't tried to butcher her the other night either. He'd used his brute strength to drag her into the water and force her face under the salty waves until her lungs had felt like two iron balls pushing against the lining of her chest. If Bart hadn't shown up when he did, she'd be dead. Her and the baby.

The baby. Growing inside her. When she'd said yes to Jackie's request, she'd never imagined it would be like this. Never dreamed an unborn infant could wrap itself so thoroughly around her heart. Never knew that before the nine months were up, she'd feel so much a part of the baby that she'd ache for the day she could hold it in her arms.

The baby belonged to Jackie and Ben, and if they were here, she would have given birth and placed the infant in their arms without ever letting them see how difficult it was to give her up. But they were dead, and the thought of never knowing or seeing the child again was ripping her apart. But she had no choice. She had to do what was best for the baby.

She walked into her bedroom, crossed to the sliding door and pushed it open. The breeze from the Gulf lifted her hair and tickled her flesh. The moon was already up, painting a steak of shimmery silver across the water.

She stepped onto the balcony. The beach was deserted, quiet, lonesome. Peaceful. Taking a deep breath, she let the fresh air fill her lungs. The baby took that time to spring to life. She kicked hard and Megan put one hand to her stomach and the other to the railing, throwing her weight against it.

The railing creaked and swung loose. Three levels below, the ground waited. The scream she heard was her own.

Chapter Eight

Bart washed the last of the frothy shaving cream from his face and dabbed a towel against his chin. He felt better after the shower, more in control, his mind back on the job he was here to do rather than on the woman. He just had to keep his cool. This, too, would pass.

Joshua Caraway should have been in custody by now and headed back to jail. It wasn't as if this was New Orleans or St. Louis where a man could change his appearance a little and blend into the masses. This was a small town, especially with the dearth of tourists.

Holding the bottle at an angle, he shook a few drops of aftershave into his hand and slapped it onto his face. A quick tug, and the towel was snug around his waist as he stepped out of the bathroom and into the guest room.

He was pulling a pair of slacks from a hanger when he heard the scream. Loud and piercing and dripping with fear. Instinctively, he grabbed his gun before tearing down the hall and toward the sound.

The door to Megan's bedroom was open and he raced through it, then stopped cold, his heart slamming against his chest. One entire section of the balcony railing had torn loose, leaving nothing between the edge of the balcony and the sand three stories below.

He forced his legs to move and propel him forward. Then he saw Megan, and the blood rushed to his head, leaving him weak. She was sagging to the side of the missing railing, head down, clutching the standing post.

He rushed to her and cradled her in his arms, holding her against him until he caught his breath enough to speak. "Are you all right?"

"Unless you count being scared half to death."

"What happened?"

"I'd just walked out to catch a breath of fresh air. The baby kicked and I grabbed the railing. The second I put my weight against it, it began swinging away from the balcony. For a minute I thought I was going with it, but I managed to grab the post and steady myself."

"Thank God. I saw the missing railing and…" He stopped talking. His voice was still shaky and he was blowing his image of tough FBI agent. "You need to lie down a minute."

"In all the years I've been coming to Pelican's Roost, I don't ever remember a railing coming loose like that. I've let the house fall into disrepair and there's no excuse for it. I'll call Fenelda tonight and have her recommend a carpenter to check out the whole place."

Disrepair or purposely sabotaged. He led her to the bed. "Lie down and take it easy. I'm going to have a look at the railing." She didn't protest though he thought she might be in better shape than he was.

He started out the door, then stopped. "Are you all right? I mean with the baby and all?"

"I think so. I'm just thinking how lucky I am. I've escaped being drowned and falling from the balcony in less than a week."

He walked onto the balcony, still shaken by how close

Megan had come to falling to her death. He was doing a damn lousy job of protecting her.

"Be careful, Bart. I don't want to lose my bodyguard at this stage of the game."

He dropped to his knees and found the place the railing had come loose. When he looked up, Megan was standing in the doorway watching him.

"My grandmother would be appalled if she knew how I've neglected the upkeep on Pelican's Roost."

"The support didn't wear out, Megan. It was deliberately cut, then fit into place so that it would give the first time someone put their weight against it."

"But who would…" She stopped in midsentence and bit her bottom lip. "The Butcher. Right?"

"He'd get my vote."

"When would he have done it? I only made up my mind to come here myself a day before I left New Orleans." She put her hands to her cheeks. "Never mind. I know when he did it. I came home from lunch the second day and knew someone had been in the house. Then I found a basket of bakery muffins on the counter and decided it was one of Grandmother's friends welcoming me back."

"Muffins. Caraway obviously learned a few new tricks during his stint in jail."

"Don't killers usually follow a pattern?"

"Not always, but when you study their past crimes, you can frequently find some way to predict what they'll do next. That's especially true of serial killers, but not necessarily true of hit men. They're usually fast and clean, with little evidence left to convict them. But Joshua blended the two. He was a hit man with a passion for torture. Before he was arrested and convicted, his hits were always massacres."

She hugged her arms about her chest. "Why would he have changed everything?"

"Ten years in jail. I imagine he spent hours planning his escape and his revenge against Ben."

"Only he wouldn't have known about me and the baby until he talked to that neighbor. Still, if he's on the run, I don't see why he would risk coming to this house and cutting the railings. Anyone could have seen him."

"Are you trying to steal my job?"

"I'm just trying to make sense of all this."

"I'd like to tell you not to worry, that you should just trust me to protect you, but I've done a poor job of it so far."

"That's not true. I'm alive because of you."

"I didn't find the cut railing."

The phone rang. He stayed until she answered it. As soon as he realized it was John, he backed out of the room. He wasn't sure what was going on between the two of them, but he knew that after her conversation with her mother, the man's name had been changed to mud.

December 14

MEGAN STOOD at the front door staring at the handyman Fenelda Shelby had recommended. The guy looked like a sex symbol right off the pages of a magazine for teenage girls. Not that he was a teenager. He was probably in his late twenties or early thirties. His blond hair was long and a little shaggy, but his skin was tanned to a deep bronze and he had the look of a bad boy in a man's body. Even the tools hanging from the leather strap at his waist had a sensual effect.

He introduced himself as Mark Cox as he sauntered

through the door. "Mrs. Shelby said you had a broken railing you needed fixed."

"I do, and I'd like you to check the other railings and the balustrade around the cupola."

"No problem. The place could use painting, too. I noticed that driving up."

"It has been a while since it's been painted. Add the cost to the estimate and give it to me. I'll make the decision later."

"Will do. Now, where's that balcony? I'll check it first. You don't want to go falling in your condition." He eyed her stomach, then looked away as if it embarrassed him.

Bart bounded down the steps in time to catch the last of the conversation. "The balcony's upstairs. I'll walk with you," he said, motioning to the stairs.

Mark followed him, keeping up with Bart's usual fast pace. "Do you live here, too?"

"I'm visiting. I was going to fix the break myself. I got as far as cutting it clean at the point where it gave way before I realized I didn't have the tools to do it right. That thing's a…" His voice drifted off as the men climbed the stairs to the third floor.

Megan stood thinking about how easily the man lied. Firmly in the role of Bart Cromwell, undercover FBI agent. He'd do whatever he had to in order to get his man.

Explain away the signs of a crime so that no one knew what was really going on at Pelican's Roost. Play the attentive lover to an unmarried pregnant woman who was as big as a baby hippo. Even decorate a Christmas tree and sing choruses of "Jingle Bells." He'd told her originally that he was good at what he did, and that had been the understatement of the year. He was terrific.

But even knowing that everything he said or did was part of the act, she found him unbelievably attractive. His talk, his walk, the way he smiled. The way his hair looked dripping wet after a shower. The way he raced down the steps as if he were ten and he was rushing off to a ball game. The way he romped and played in the surf. Even his determination to make a monster called The Butcher pay for his crime.

But it was all a ruse, a fake identity created by the FBI. Bart Cromwell only existed in the here and now.

Joshua Caraway, however, seemed to live on forever.

December 16

BART PULLED UP in front of Penny and Tom Drummonds's house just before eight. The driveway was already full and there were a couple of cars parked on the street. "Looks like the little get-together turned into a big party."

"Penny was always the social organizer."

"How well do you know her?"

"I went to high school here my junior and senior years. Mom was off doing some kind of dancing project in Spain. She was only supposed to be gone for three months, but she met some guy who was the love of her life at that point, divorced husband number three and stayed in Spain for a few years."

"And you were stuck in Orange Beach while she toured Spain."

"I was thankful. It was the first time I ever got to go to one school for more than a year, and the first time I made real friends. Jackie and I were almost inseparable. It was funny the way we hit it off. She was the closest thing to a sister I ever had."

"I'm sure your grandmother was happy about that."

"Not at first. I got the impression she didn't approve of our being so close, but she warmed up as time went on. Which is more than Jackie's mom did. Right until I moved away, I had the feeling she didn't like me around. I think she was jealous of our relationship. She and Jackie had been very close. Her dad was always nice, though. He never said much when I was around, but he wasn't unfriendly."

"But they're both dead now," he said. "Her father was killed six years ago in a flash flood while camping in the Northwest. Her mother died a few years later of cancer."

"I forget you know everything about me and Jackie. Why do you even bother to ask me questions?"

"Your version's always more interesting than the cut-and-dried one I get from the guys in research."

Bart stared in the rearview mirror as a blue compact pulled up behind them. "I guess we better make our grand entrance. People will be wondering what we're doing in the car for so long."

"I'm ready if you are, boyfriend."

Boyfriend. The job had become harder and harder over the past two days. Tonight, he'd really be put to the test. Looking convincing to the people at the party would be easy. The test would come in trying not to let Megan know that the feelings he was supposed to be faking were all too real.

He'd given up on pretending they didn't exist or in trying to understand the attraction. She was pregnant. She'd given him no reason to think she was interested in him. It was against policy. It had never happened before when he was on a case.

Nonetheless, he'd fallen for her and romance and case-work were as dangerous as gasoline in the hands of an arsonist. So this time he'd find out what kind of actor he really was.

"TWINS. They are so cute." Megan flipped through the pictures Alice Leaderman had pulled from her wallet. "How old are they?"

"Six. In first grade already. I miss my babies. I wanted more, but Bill put his foot down. He said I was liable to have triplets next time, and he'd never make enough money to feed them."

"You guys are putting me to shame," Megan said. "You have kids in school and I haven't even married yet."

"You were always too serious-minded for romance, Megan."

So that's how they saw her. Maybe they were right. The only guy she'd ever dated seriously was John, and at the first sign of trouble, she'd broken up with him and never looked back.

She turned to one of the other old classmates who'd joined their cluster. "What about you, Dorothy. You always said you'd never get married. You were going to be a doctor and make scads of money."

"God, do you remember that?"

"We all remember that." The chorus was followed by a round of laughter.

"I'm very married. Instead of the medical field, I'm working at the library, volunteer. Amos sells real estate. That's how I met him. My parents invested in a beach condo to supplement their retirement income, and I invested in Amos. That's him over there in the blue shirt and jeans talking to your guy, Megan. Who, by the way, is some hunk."

Megan turned to get a look at Amos, but it was Bart

she noticed. He was mingling and mixing, laughing and talking as if he'd known these people all his life instead of for the last two hours. He was probably glad to get out and socialize with someone besides her.

"So where did you meet this hunk?" Alice asked.

"We were classmates together back at Auburn." The lie bothered her, grew thick on her tongue. No matter how much practice she got, she'd never be as good at this as Bart was. She turned her gaze to a crystal reindeer on a nearby table.

"She hadn't seen him since college and then he just waltzed back into her life last week," Penny said. "They didn't even recognize each other. Can you believe it? Now he looks at her the way my Tom looks at that boat at the marina that he's been panting after."

Alice slid the wallet into her pocket. "What does he think about you being a surrogate mother?"

"We haven't talked about it much. There's no point in talking at this stage. It's done."

"I don't think I have one friend who'd do that for me," Dorothy said.

"Definitely not in this group," they all agreed, once more breaking into easy laughter.

"I can't imagine what it would be like to give birth and then go home empty-handed and empty-hearted," Dorothy said, eyeing Megan's protruding belly. "I hope the mother knows what a dear you are for doing this."

The words were like daggers in Megan's heart, but Dorothy had no way of knowing just how cruelly her words hit home.

"Okay, we're getting far too deep for a party," Penny announced. "I say we grab the men and drag them to the deck for some dancing. I want to twirl under the stars before Tom has one too many cups of eggnog."

"Yes, and I want to dance with Megan's beau," Alice added. "It's been far too long since I've gotten to put my arms around a hard body."

Megan pushed to her feet and joined them. As long as the conversation was on something other than her pregnancy, she could join in the laughter with the rest of them. Old friends. Relaxed. Laughing. In this atmosphere it was difficult to believe a killer walked the back streets of Orange Beach, hid in the sand dunes, waiting for a chance to kill her. Wherever he was, he must be anxious to finish the job and disappear.

Killers didn't belong in Orange Beach, especially at Christmastime.

MEGAN STROLLED onto the deck with Bart, arm in arm, playing the role handed to them by fate. The night was warm for December and Penny's deck was sheltered from the cool breeze that blew constantly across the sandy beach surrounding Pelican's Roost.

A few couples were dancing to a tune with a beat a lot faster than Megan was moving these days. Still, she got into the rhythm, shaking her shoulders and humming along.

"Would you like to dance?" Bart asked.

"I would *love* to dance. Can you come back and ask me about this time next month?"

"I can probably arrange that, if I can find you. Where will you be? London? Sydney? Johannesburg?"

"Or New Orleans." She raised on tiptoe and put her mouth close to his ear. "Just don't bring any of your killer friends with you next time." She noticed Dorothy watching her and smiling, no doubt sure Megan was whispering some indecent proposal in his ear.

"I promise to come alone," he whispered back, his

breath hot on her face and sending shivers of pleasure dancing up her spine. "If you can't dance, how about some fruit punch?"

"That sounds good."

"I'll be right back, so don't boogie off with any other guy while I'm gone."

He disappeared through the door and she settled onto the bench that bordered the deck. Christmas lights were strung in the branches of two nearby pine trees and baskets of red poinsettias hung from hooks above the deck. Not the kind of glitzy holiday extravaganzas she'd be attending if she were back in the corporate-world social whirl, but cozy and intimate. She'd forgotten how much fun parties like this could be.

Several of the guys and a couple of the ladies were already feeling their Christmas spirits, talking and laughing louder than usual and doing a few dance steps she bet they didn't try when they were sober.

The music changed from rock to a two-steppin' country tune as Bart returned with her punch. Penny sidled up next to him as he slipped the cup into Megan's hands.

"May I borrow him for a dance, Megan? Tom's inside sharing tales with Amos about the ones that got away."

"Be my guest."

Bart hesitated.

"Go on," she said, nudging him toward Penny. "Just don't twirl her under the mistletoe. I'll be keeping my eye on you."

She watched as the two danced away. She wasn't jealous, but she was a tad envious. It had been months since she'd felt as graceful as they looked circling the floor, their steps in perfect rhythm. Her gaze stayed on Bart. Tough, gentle and a good dancer. And single. She never ran into men like that in New Orleans, not that she had time to go out looking.

The song ended and a new one started. An oldie but goodie, one she'd first heard when her grandmother used to put a stack of records on her old phonograph. "All about the possibility of never meeting again." She sang along softly, lost in memories until Bart appeared in front of her.

"My dad says you should always dance with the one who brung you, so may I have this dance?"

"You are joking, aren't you? You couldn't get within a foot of me."

"We'll improvise." He took her arm and tugged her to her feet.

"I'll wobble like a duck out of water. People will stare."

"That's their problem." He took her in his arms and she had no choice but to follow his lead or make a scene. And she'd never been one to make a scene.

He didn't hold her close, but still she was keenly aware of her hand in his and of his other hand at her waist. The awkwardness faded, and moving to the music, she felt as if she was gliding across the room, though she knew it wouldn't look that way to anyone else. She closed her eyes, let the danger slip into a back corner of her mind. She was a woman dancing with a tall, dark stranger who was not what he seemed to be.

The concept was provocative, the feelings surging through her erotic and seductive. She forgot everything and let herself melt into the moment. When the song ended, she trembled, from disappointment and the unexpected heat that had crept into every cell of her body.

He looked up. "What do you know? We stopped right under the mistletoe." His lips touched hers. The kiss was tentative at first, but when she responded, he deepened the kiss, taking her mouth hungrily. Her arms wrapped around his neck and she held on as emotions she hadn't felt in a long, long time rocked inside her. When he broke away, she realized everyone was watching them.

Heat flushed her cheeks as Bart led her off to the edge of the deck to cheers from the women—and jeers from the men since Bart had made them look bad in front of their wives.

If it bothered him at all, he didn't show it. He joked right along with them, saying it wasn't his fault if they couldn't cut it.

Whatever else Bart Cromwell was, he was a very good kisser. Unless this was just another phase of the hormone imbalance that went along with pregnancy, a temporary feeling of euphoria, of heightened emotions from a man's touch, from a meaningless kiss.

They sat the next one out, hand in hand on the bench at the edge of the deck. It was hard to imagine that her world could seem this right, when it was spinning on an axis bound for collision with a killer.

THE SAND WAS COOL to the man's bare feet as he made his way along the clusters of sea oats and sand dunes half a mile from the Lancaster house. He couldn't even see the roofline of the old relic from here. It was blocked by the towering condos. But he knew every line of the place.

Megan Lancaster was never alone now. That stupid gold-digger boyfriend was around every minute, pretending to fall head over heels for a woman whose body was all stretched out of proportion. He wouldn't think a professional woman like Megan Lancaster would be that gullible, but some women were like that. Throw them a little attention, make a few idle promises and they'd do any-thing you wanted.

He'd had his share of women, all ages, all colors, all creeds, but nothing he'd done with them gave him the kind of thrill that killing did. It was the optimum thrill, the ultimate arousal.

He wouldn't be able to make it look like an accident the way he'd planned. There was no time for that now that the loose railing and the drowning had been foiled. Just a simple bullet through the head and then it would all be over. She'd be home soon. And when she arrived, he'd be waiting—despite her boyfriend.

He touched his hand to the pistol. One quick click and it would all be over. *Bang. Bang.* And he'd win the jack-pot.

To the victor went the spoils.

Chapter Nine

The kiss stayed on Megan's mind as they drove back to the beach house. It had been sizzling and romantic, no doubt convincing her friends in Orange Beach that there was something magical between her and Bart. He almost had her believing it, and she never reacted to men like this. The only possible explanations were the pregnancy and the danger she'd been hurled into over the past few days.

Add to those the fact that she was with him every waking moment. He was the first person she saw in the morning, the last person before she closed her eyes at night. When she was upset, he managed to make her laugh. When she wanted to talk, he listened.

But it wasn't merely familiarity, a bond wrought from necessity, that was growing inside her. It was something potent, carnal, earthy. Feelings she'd never had before and that were almost as frightening as the madman who'd become the would-be assassin of the baby growing inside her.

Even now, just sitting beside Bart in the car, her heart beat a little faster and her emotions seemed charged with a kind of psychic energy that made the stars seem brighter, the air clearer, her senses more keen than they'd been in a long, long time.

He pulled off the road and drove down the narrow driveway that led to the house, but stopped short of his usual parking space. Instead, he parked so that they had a clear view of the beach. The moon split the water with a silver steak and then danced along the whitecaps in a shimmery glow. She lowered her window so that she could breathe the salty air and listen to the rhythmic chant of the waves breaking onto the sandy shore.

Bart killed the engine. "It's easy to see why you kept this place even though you get to come back here so seldom. You must miss it."

"Most days I don't have time to miss it. I'm usually frantically organizing meetings or verifying facts or going over notes. For both John and I, it's nonstop."

"He must be managing without you now."

"Not well. That's why he calls so often and why he pulled that ridiculous trick, calling my mother to make certain I don't decide to keep the baby."

"Are your mother and John friends as well?"

"The only time he met her was at my grandmother's funeral. We were dating at the time, and he stayed here at Pelican's Roost with us. Mother charmed the socks off him, of course. What can I say? She has a way with men." She squirmed in her seat trying to get more comfortable. "If we're going to sit here and watch the moonlight shimmer across the water, can't we discuss something more pleasant?"

"What would you like to talk about?"

"You. The real you—not the Bart Cromwell who only goes back a couple of weeks."

He eased his seat back, put his hand behind his head

and leaned against the headrest. "There's not much to tell. When I'm not working, I'm your average guy."

Sexy. Intelligent. Thoughtful. Obviously his definition of average differed from hers. "What happened between you and your wife."

"We met, fell in love in a fevered rush, got married and then she realized I wasn't the exciting FBI agent she'd imagined."

"You make it sound so cut-and-dried."

"One of my shortcomings. I don't deal well with failure. But actually, the marriage had its moments. They were just too few and far between for her. Apparently she got tired of living alone when I was off on assignment."

"Did she ask you to give up your job?"

"Nope. She just found a replacement."

"Is that what she told you?"

"She didn't tell me anything. That would have been too simple and downright kind compared to the way she delivered the message. I came home early from an assignment and found her in our bed in the middle of the day. She wasn't alone."

"How dreadful! You must have been devastated."

"At the time, I was mostly furious. She thought I was going to draw my gun and shoot him."

"How did you handle it?"

"I turned around and walked out. Went out and tied on the biggest drunk of my life. When I sobered up, I went home, packed my clothes and got the hell out of Dodge. It was a week before I calmed down enough to talk to her."

"And I was the one who suggested we should talk about something pleasant."

"This wasn't it, but the breakup was five years ago. I'm past the anger and the hurt, though I expect the dis-

illusionment of something like that sticks with a man forever. I know I'm not the most trusting man where women
are concerned.''

"How long had you been married?"

"Eleven months, give or take a few days. Five, to be
exact. But who's counting?"

"And you never married again?"

"Never came close. Some men just aren't meant to be
married. I'm one of them.''

"That's odd. I think the same thing about myself sometimes. The whole idea of being so joined with another
human being that you lose part of your identity is frightening. When I think of it, I tend to panic and run for
cover.''

"Is that why you broke off your engagement with
John?"

"I panicked. I won't deny that. I felt that if I was ever
going to get married, it was time. I even thought John was
the right man. We're both so professionally driven, but
when it came down to going through with the ceremony,
I couldn't do it.''

"Maybe you didn't love him."

"I'm not even sure I know what love is, at least not
that kind of love. I know I didn't feel about John the way
Jackie felt about Ben. I don't blame that on John. I think
I probably lack the ability to fall in love that completely.''

"I wouldn't give up on it yet. Some guy might come
along and ring all of your bells.''

"If he does, I hope he kisses the way you do." She bit
her bottom lip and wondered how she'd let that slip out.

He lifted his head and turned to meet her gaze. "A kiss
takes two.''

"I guess that's something even a pregnant woman can
do.''

"You're really hung up on this pregnant stuff. Being pregnant doesn't make you a freak. If anything, it makes you more a woman."

"I don't think I'm a freak. Just a realist. I know what men notice first in a woman. Breasts and behinds, to put it nicely."

"You're right. That is what men notice first. It's the allure, the thing that gets their attention. And if you're looking to be picked up in a bar or at a party, it definitely helps if you're built and looking hot."

He stretched his arm along the back of her seat. His hand touched her hair, and she felt her breath catch and then slowly release, but she didn't look away.

"But once a man gets to know a woman, he sees past all of that. You have more going for you pregnant than most women do on the best night of their lives."

He eased closer, and she felt the sizzle deep inside her. For a second, she thought he was going to kiss her again, but at the last second he pulled away and planted both hands on the wheel, wrapping his fingers around it.

"Are you ready to go in?" he asked without moving his stare from the beach and stretch of Gulf in front of them.

"I'm ready."

He pushed down on the door handle, then stopped. "Don't get out of the car, Megan." His voice delivered the strain that was evidenced in the set of his jaw and the lines of his face. He pulled a gun from the holster beneath his jacket.

"What is it?"

"A shadow, in that thick cluster of sea oats just past the corner of the house. See. It moved again."

"Joshua Caraway." The name was only a whisper on

her lips, but the frigid freight that it carried struck straight for the heart.

"I'm going to pull the car into the garage," he said, "to our usual parking spot. I want you to stay in the car and keep your head down."

"He'll have a gun, too, Bart."

"I'm sure he will. He's likely been standing there watching us, impatiently waiting for you to step out of the car or to start up the steps so that he has a clear shot at you. That's why we'll make sure he doesn't get that chance."

He eased the car into gear, then backed it into the covered parking spot, slowly, as if they had all the time in the world, as if a man weren't hidden in the swaying stalks of the sea oats waiting to kill them.

"You can't just walk out there and face a man with a gun." Her voice shook. She was shaking, her body rocking with fear.

"That's what I get paid to do. It's the reason I'm here. I'm leaving the key in the ignition. If you hear gunshots, drive away as fast as you can. Go to the Waffle House and wait for me inside. I'll call you on the cell phone when it's safe to return."

"And what if you don't call? What if you're lying here bleeding to death?"

"Go to the police and have them contact the FBI. But give me half an hour. I may have to chase him down."

"But I can't—"

"You can and you will. You have a baby to think of."

A second later, he slid out of the car, leaving her to wait and worry. She could see the tenseness in his face and in the set of his jaw, but she didn't glimpse any sign of the fear and dread that choked her breath away.

This was who he was, FBI agent on the job, a man who

faced danger the way she faced a big merger. And the fear churning inside her must be what it was like for any woman who married him. Month after month, assignment after assignment.

No wonder his first wife had only lasted eleven months. Eleven months of feeling the way she did as she watched him walk away from the car, gun in hand, would seem like a lifetime.

BART PAUSED at the edge of the house. Once he left the cover of the house's overhang and started walking up the steps, he'd have no cover. He'd have to play this carefully, force Joshua into the open. He stepped to the edge, enough so he could see, not enough to become a sitting duck.

"I know you're out there, Caraway. Throw down your gun and step out into the open with your hands in the air."

A bullet shattered the wood just above his head, sending splinters flying into his face. It had missed him by inches. Adrenaline shot through him but didn't override the caution. He had no hankering to wind up a dead man.

Joshua fired again, and this time the bullet ricocheted off the third step. He was firing too soon, not waiting for a clear shot. This wasn't at all like The Butcher. The years in prison must have dulled his senses.

Keeping his back to the wall, he moved to the other side of the house and eased his way down the side and toward the beach, knowing that Megan had not started the car and driven away as he'd instructed. So much for the authority of the FBI. This meant he'd have to make sure he got Joshua before the man got him and went gunning for Megan.

He didn't have as good a view of Joshua's position

from where he was standing now, but Caraway didn't have as open a shot either. He peeked around the side of the house and stuck the gun in plain view, his finger on the trigger. "Stand in the clearing and throw down your gun."

There was nothing. Not a sound. Not a movement.

"I'm warning you, Caraway. Unless you step out and throw down your gun, I'll shoot."

Damn. Still nothing. Even a bullet would be welcome now, as long as it missed him. Then he'd at least know Joshua hadn't changed his position. He hated to just start shooting without a clear target.

He fired once, just over the tops of the sea oats. The bullet cracked through the night, and still there was no movement. Either Joshua was waiting coolly for him to step into the open so that he could gun him down or else he'd decided to wait for his real target before he killed again.

Cautiously, he made his way across the front of the house, staying in the shadows as much as he could. When he was close enough, he made a run for the nearest sand dune, clearing the distance in seconds and crouching behind it. He had a good view of the sea oats from here, but saw no sign of human shadows. He fired again, but even as he did, he knew it was useless.

While he'd moved into position, Caraway had escaped the scene. Damn. He'd been this close to having him, and the man had vanished as quickly and as silently as the moon slipping behind a cloud. And then he saw the dark figure ducking in and out of the shadows and clusters of sea oats as he raced away.

He ran after the man, his shoes sinking with each step and filling with sand, but there was no time to shed them. He was fast, but Caraway's head start gave him the advantage. Lungs burning, he pushed himself to the limit, only to lose sight of Caraway once he reached the section of the beach where the parade of high-rise condominiums practically met the sea.

He searched for as long as he dared stay away from Megan, fearing that somehow Joshua would double back and find her unprotected. He headed back to Pelican's Roost at the same steady speed.

He slowed, feeling a surge of relief as he reached the house and saw her standing on the first balcony. He wasn't sure how long Megan could keep this up, enduring one deadly stressor after another with the baby almost due. He expected every new crisis to send her into early labor—or at the very least hysterics—but so far she was hanging in there with the tenacity of a steel hook.

But as strong as she was, that was how weak he was growing in the relationship department. The kiss tonight had proven that. He was falling so hard it would take a crane to right him again when this was over. The really scary part was that he knew she felt the same attraction.

Except it was a lose-lose situation. Even if it wasn't against every written and unwritten rule in the book to fall for someone you were protecting, he wasn't fool enough to think a woman like her would want a man like him when the crisis was over.

At best, they could have a brief affair. Of course, that was all either of them were interested in. She'd said herself, she wasn't the marrying kind, and he definitely had nothing to offer a woman like Megan.

A brief affair with a woman about to deliver a baby.

Who was he fooling?

He just had to get through this, get his man and keep his hands off the woman. He'd done it dozens of times before. How hard could it be to do it once more?

MEGAN STOOD on the balcony, her heart in her throat as she watched Bart trudge up the incline that led from the beach to the house. He was apparently unhurt, but that didn't change the way she'd felt a few minutes ago when she'd sat in the car and listened to the cracking of gunfire. Didn't wipe away the terror she'd felt, not knowing if Bart was dead or alive.

But finally, the fear and excruciating anxiety had given her the strength to make the decision she should have made a long time ago. She wouldn't stay here and be dangled out as bait, couldn't chance having all of them killed while the FBI played deadly games with a madman.

She'd drive to Mobile and check into a hotel suite under an assumed name and hire a bodyguard to stand guard over the room. Someone with no agenda except to keep her and the baby safe.

If the FBI wanted to catch Joshua Caraway, they'd do it without her. And this time she wouldn't be swayed by her emotions and her allegiance to her dead friend. She was carrying Jackie's baby and that was all she could handle. Most of all she wouldn't be forced to watch while Bart engaged in gunplay with a killer. She wouldn't be the one responsible for him getting shot and maybe killed.

She splayed her hand across her belly, gathering comfort from the innocence that grew in her womb. "It's going to be just you and me, sweetie."

And I'll pray that Bart Cromwell stays alive in the meantime.

BART WATCHED MEGAN take the stirs to her bedroom. He was standing in the same spot, struggling to deal with Megan's announcement, when his phone rang. He could understand her fear and her wanting to run, but as soon as the dust settled from the latest attack, he'd be able to talk some sense into her.

"You must be psychic," Bart said as soon as Luke Powell identified himself. I was just about to call you."

"I'm glad I beat you to it. I have good news."

"If it's about a Caraway sighting in St. Louis, you can forget it."

"It's not a siting, Bart. He's in custody. Two cops arrested him tonight in Chicago. It's all over."

"It's not over in Orange Beach. There was another attempt on Megan's life just minutes ago."

"It wasn't Joshua Caraway. I can guarantee you that."

"Then he's hired someone to kill Megan or called in a favor."

"If Joshua Caraway was going to have someone else do his dirty work for him, he wouldn't have waited until he was out of jail to do it. He's got more connections in the criminal underground than I've got gray hairs."

"I don't know why he's hired someone now, but I'm telling you that he has."

"That's an interesting theory, but we don't have squat to back it up."

"I have a killer in the Orange Beach area and he has Megan Lancaster targeted at his victim."

"I don't know what you've walked into down there, Bart, but the evidence indicates it has nothing to do with our case against Joshua Caraway. He's not the man who attacked her tonight and we have no real reason to believe he was behind the explosion that killed the Brewsters."

"This can't be coincidence."

"No, but it may have nothing to do with Joshua Caraway. We have to consider the possibility that this is about Megan Lancaster and Jackie Brewster. They could have been into anything. Megan travels all over the world on a regular basis and she has her inheritance from her grandmother to fund anything, legal or illegal, that she wants to dabble in. You knew that going in.''

''What I know right now is that she's not smuggling or involved in any other kind of criminal activity. She's about to deliver a baby any day now, and the odds she can keep escaping her killer are going down fast.''

''I know I don't have to tell you this, Cromwell, but with Joshua Caraway under arrest, we no longer have a legitimate interest in Megan Lancaster or the problems in Orange Beach. As long as we suspected Caraway of going after a witness and then carrying his death sentence across state lines to find Megan Lancaster, we had reason to go after him. Now he's in custody.''

''You're not suggesting I just walk off the job.''

''I'm telling you that I can't keep this case open more than a few more days unless there's some real indication we have a right to be there.''

''I can't leave Megan unprotected.''

''You can go with her to the police, tell them what you know and encourage them to furnish protection.''

''You know I'm not dropping this case until it's finished.''

''We're not superheroes, Cromwell. We can't just push our way into every crime that involves a nice pregnant woman just because we think we can do it better than the local authorities.''

''What if they ask for our help?''

''If they ask, we can take it under consideration.''

''And by then Megan and her unborn child will be dead,'' he said emotionally. ''I'll tell you what, if it comes to that, if the bureau drops this case, you can consider me on leave until I find the man responsible for the attempts on her life.''

"I don't know what's going on between you and this woman, and I don't want to know. I'll hold the case open as long as I can. After that, you're on your own, but if it comes to that, you have to level with her. You can't let her think you're acting as an undercover agent."

"I understand."

"Don't let this woman mess with your mind. Being pregnant doesn't make a woman a saint."

"Is that your official advice?"

"No, that's from the private mouth of Luke Powell. My official advice is turn this over to the local authorities and head home."

"I'll think about it."

"Keep me posted."

"Yeah, look, I gotta run. I'll get back with you in the morning."

He broke the connection. If he had any sense at all, he'd do exactly what his boss had suggested, especially since Megan was telling him she'd had enough of his protection. But whether she wanted him or not, he wasn't going anywhere without her until he knew she was safe.

MEGAN SAT on the side of her bed staring out into the night and attempting to assimilate the new information Bart had thrown at her, the continuing saga of a nightmare that wouldn't quit. She turned to face him. "If Joshua Caraway is in jail, then it shouldn't matter if I just go check into a hotel until the baby's born."

"My job is to protect you."

"Then you should be glad I'm leaving. Your job will be concluded." This might be merely a job to him, but she couldn't keep facing the kind of fear she'd known tonight. Hearing the deafening crack of gunfire but not knowing if he'd been hit, if he was lying in a pool of his own blood dying a slow death or possibly being butchered by a knife-wielding monster. Wondering if she and the baby would be next.

"Someone wants you dead, Megan. If it's not Joshua Caraway, then it's someone else. You checking into a hotel in Mobile won't make him go away."

"I can't comprehend the implications of this tonight, Bart. I'm exhausted and body weary from all that's happened. I only want to do is crawl into my bed, stretch out between the sheets and sleep."

"Fine. We can talk in the morning."

"We can talk until we're blue in the face, but we're not going to come up with some bizarre murderous plot that involves Jackie and me. There is no reason for anyone to want to kill me except the man that you say is back in custody."

"I have some ideas, a new plan I'd like to put in operation immediately."

She shook her head. "In the morning, Bart. If there is a morning. Now I'm going to wash my face, brush my teeth and crash. And if the phone rings before 10:00 a.m., I'm going to rip the cord from the wall."

He took her hand and tugged her to a standing position. It was difficult to believe that earlier tonight they had been dancing on Penny's deck. That he had kissed her underneath a sprig of mistletoe and that he'd felt the thrill in every part of his body.

She looked up at him. "After this, if I ever get a fortune cookie that says I'm going to meet a tall, dark, handsome stranger, I'm going to flush the message down the toilet."

"Handsome, huh?"

She managed a smile. "That was the conclusion of the women at the party."

"Look at it this way, think of all the excitement you'd have missed if I hadn't walked into your life."

"Excitement is closing a big deal, finding a gorgeous dress on sale, doing a perfect run down a difficult ski slope. It is not being hunted by a madman. I rest my case. The fortune goes down the sewer."

"Same here. If my fortune says I'm going to meet a warm, intelligent, beautiful pregnant woman who'll lure me away to a wonderful house in paradise, I'll grind it up and crush it under my feet."

"Beautiful, huh?"

"Absolutely." He trailed a finger down her cheek. "If you need me tonight, just call. I'm a light sleeper."

The fear quotient kicked in again. "You don't think the killer will return tonight, do you?"

"I doubt it. I imagine he's back at the drawing board thinking up a new plan. If he does, the doors and windows are bolted, and there's no moving silently in this house. You get some rest. Trust me, I hear every creak and rattle."

"Good," she agreed. "But that still doesn't mean I'm going to go along with your plans tomorrow. I only promise to hear them out."

"Fair enough." He hesitated.

"Is there something else?"

"About that kiss tonight."

"You don't need to explain or apologize for the kiss. I know it was part of the act, a way to convince everyone we're really lovers."

"No." His gaze met hers and a nervous half smile tugged at his lips. "The kiss had nothing to do with Bart Cromwell or with the case. I just thought you should know."

Before she had a chance to comment, he was gone. She

touched her fingers to her lips, and the emotions she'd felt under the mistletoe came back again in a burst of heat that penetrated every part of her body.

She might be in deep trouble, but she wasn't dead yet. She stared at her bulging stomach in the mirror. "What do you think, sweetie. Is he a keeper or what? Not that I'm in the market for a keeper, but if I was, he'd move to the top of my list."

The little angel balled into a knot. Megan lightly stroked her stomach. "I'll take that as a vote of approval."

Not that it mattered. Not that anything mattered now except keeping the baby safe. A baby she already loved more than life itself. A baby she'd have to give away as soon as she was born. The same way Bart Cromwell would disappear from her life as soon as her would-be killer was arrested. Maybe sooner, if she followed her instincts.

Wasn't there anything fair about life? She already knew the answer to that. If life was fair, Jackie would be here waiting for the birth of her baby girl.

And Megan would be sleeping in Bart Cromwell's arms tonight.

Chapter Ten

December 17

Megan stared out the window of the cozy breakfast nook, sipping a glass of fresh-squeezed orange juice while Bart downed his third cup of coffee. Dozens of sea gulls swarmed a preschool tyke as he danced across the sand, throwing bread crumbs over his head. Each time a bird caught one of the tidbits in mid-air, the boy jumped up and down and squealed. Megan soaked up the scene—a shred of normalcy in world gone mad.

Bart leaned against the window frame. "I haven't seen so many people on the beach since I've been here."

"It's Saturday and the weather is absolutely gorgeous," she said. "That always brings folks out from the inland cities. There's a big arts and craft show in Fairhope this weekend as well. Sandra Birney called and asked if I wanted to go with her."

"And if it weren't for this mess, you could," he answered, aggravation heavy in his voice. "It would be a good outing for you."

"I'm not sure I'm up to it, though I did rest well last night."

Bart sat his coffee mug on the windowsill and raked his fingers through his tousled hair. "I'm glad someone slept well. I tossed and turned and wrestled with sick possibilities. If it's not Joshua Caraway who's behind the attacks on your life, then I don't have a single suspect. Still, it's hard to imagine that it was coincidence that an explosion killed Ben and Jackie right before a killer started stalking you. That would mean it was blind luck that brought me into your life just in time to save you from being drowned the other night."

"My grandmother would call it the work of angels."

"I think I would have liked your grandmother."

"I'm sure you would have. There was nothing not to like about her."

"Did your mother feel the same way about her?"

"Not always. I remember hearing them argue when I was growing up, mostly when they thought I was asleep."

"What kinds of things did they argue about?"

With anyone else, she'd have taken the question for idle curiosity, but she knew Bart too well now to believe that. He was always on the job, searching for the missing links, the unexpected clues that would lead him to vital information.

"Mostly my mother's lifestyle. Grandmother thought she should settle in one place and make a home for me. And Grandmother hated the fact that Mother had a steady stream of lovers moving in and out of her life. She was sure it was corrupting my morals."

"Looks like she didn't have to worry about that."

"How would you know? I may have a stream of lovers myself. I could have lived with dozens of men."

"Have you?"

"No. I wouldn't even move in with John when we were

planning to marry. I'm not sure I'll ever be ready to share my life that completely with another human being."

"You're living with me now."

And so she was. And growing more used to him by the hour. Thirty-one, and never really been in love, never met a man she'd trusted enough to let him into the deep chambers of her heart and soul. Her grandmother had worried that she'd adopt her mother's penchant for shallow love affairs. Instead she'd gone the other way, blocked out love and commitment completely.

Mothers and their daughters. One way or another, for good or for bad, the influence always took hold.

Bart wrapped his arms around her, resting his hands on the rounded bulge of her stomach. "The little one seems quiet this morning."

"She is. Getting ready for her big birth experience, I guess."

"I'm excited about it myself."

The man was amazing. She'd feared at first that he had some kind of fetish for out-of-shape women. Always finding a reason to discredit the fact that he found her desirable. But it was her problem. Not his.

"Tell me about Jackie Brewster," he said, jumping back into the conversation. "Were the two of you always close?"

"We were always there for one another, ever since high school, but we didn't see that much of each other over the last few years. She was busy with Ben and I was busy with my job. The great thing was that no matter how long we went between visits, the minute we saw each other or talked to each other, it was just like old times."

"Did you ever work together?"

"No."

"What about business ventures?" he asked. "Did you lend her money or sign off on any loans."

"She never asked."

"Just a good friend." Bart's brows furrowed. "So let's skip to John Hardison. Tell me all about your telephoning coworker."

"What kind of things do you want to know?"

"What's he like. His personality, moods, temperament. Is he over you? Is he jealous?"

She shook her head and pulled away. "Does he want me dead?"

"I didn't ask that."

"But you're thinking it. I can't do this, Bart. I can't start looking at every person I know and wondering if they're the one who wants me dead."

"I don't see how you're going to avoid it. If it's not Joshua Caraway who wants you dead—and I'm still not totally convinced that he's not behind this—then it's someone else. Either way we have to find them and stop them."

"I don't. I can't. I'm leaving Pelican's Roost. I can't keep playing hide and seek with a killer when I'm this close to my delivery date."

"I've told you before, Megan. Leaving Pelican's Roost won't change anything."

"It will for me."

He took her hands in his. "I know how hard this is on you, Megan, but I can't let you go off by yourself. I'm in this with you. There's no other way."

"You may be in this with me, but it's not the same. Your motive is different. I can understand that. You find offenders and put them away. It's who you are, what you do."

"Not this time, Megan. It's more."

"I don't want more. Not now."

He grimaced and exhaled sharply. "What are you afraid of, Megan? A killer or the fact that you liked it when I kissed you?"

"Please, Bart. Don't do this." She tried to pull away, but he kept a firm grip on her hand. "All I can think about now is having this baby and keeping it safe."

"Then we do have different motives. I'm thinking about both of you, and I know that neither of you will be safe until the man who's out to kill you is either dead himself or in jail."

The waters of the Gulf sparkled like dancing jewels in the bright sunlight, and yet her insides were a frigid mass, like ice cubes that started to melt and then began to freeze into one solid block.

"I have a plan, Megan, but we have to be here to carry it out. You don't have to ever step outside the door."

"I'll be a prisoner."

"That's the same thing you're talking about, except you want to be a prisoner away from everything familiar, away from friends, away from your doctor. Away from a man who cares about you and will do anything in his power to keep you alive."

He wrapped his arms around her and held her as close as her body would allow. The ice inside her began to melt. A heated warmth mingled with the strength and determination that seemed to flow from his body to hers.

"Let's hear the plan," she said, knowing that he'd already won the battle.

"Over breakfast."

BART PUSHED his empty breakfast plate away. In its place, he spread a sheet of paper separated into three columns. "In the first column we have facts that we know." He tapped the eraser end of a pencil against the paper. "Number one, Joshua Caraway broke out of jail seven weeks ago. He was picked up last night in Illinois and is on his way back to prison."

No wonder the man hadn't slept last night. He'd been up making charts and lists. She stood and carried the plates to the sink. "Keep reading. I absorb better when my hands are busy."

"Fact number two. Ben and Jackie Brewster were killed in an explosion in their home five weeks ago."

"I notice you didn't mention that you're convinced the explosion was deliberate."

"That's in the likely-possibility column. Fact three, the Brewster's next-door neighbor told me that a surrogate mother was about to give birth to a baby whose biological parents were Jackie and Ben."

"And the neighbor admitted she had told someone else the same story?" She held the plates under a spray of cool water and brushed away the bits of toast remaining on Ben's plate.

"The woman was still in shock when I talked to her. She blurted out that information without thinking, and she could have done the same with other people without even realizing it.

"Fact four. Jackie's gynecologist's office was broken into."

"And nothing was taken but drugs."

"Nonetheless, her medical records could have been read, and your name was listed as the surrogate parent.

"Fact five. Joshua Caraway vowed that he'd get back at Ben one day by killing him and every member of his family."

She poured dishwasher detergent into the machine. "Only Joshua Caraway is back in jail."

Grabbing a dish cloth, she went to work wiping the top of the range and all the cabinets, moving things as she went to get to every corner. Fenelda would be in to clean tomorrow, but she had to stay busy, had to have something to do with her hands to keep from pounding them into the wall.

He stood up and went to stare out the window. "So unless Caraway's merely orchestrating this and letting someone else do the dirty work for him—and that's extremely unlikely—we have to look at the possibility that your would-be killer is totally unrelated to the deaths of Jackie and Ben."

"Why would anyone want to kill me, especially here in Orange Beach? I live in New Orleans. We have one of the highest murder rates per capita in the United States and I've never had so much as my purse snatched there."

"But someone does want you dead. The who and the why are what we have to find out."

"And this must bring us to the plan that you talked about."

"I don't have any easy answers. There's no formula in the FBI handbook that we can just follow and come up with a killer."

"So what do you suggest?"

"We have to sit down together and go over every aspect of your life, past and present. The first option is to see who would benefit from your death. If we don't come up with anything there, we look at everyone you know, every business dealing you've had, every relationship you've been in, including anything that you and Jackie ever did together."

Every aspect of her life. Dig into the past when she'd spent years trying to bury it. "That could take forever."

"We'll start with the elimination method. Not everyone

will have the means and the opportunity. And there's always the possibility we can catch the man in the act." He walked over and leaned against the counter. "There is one other thing I have to tell you."

"There's more?" She circled the bulge of her stomach with her arms. "Do you hear that, little one? There's more. You may want to come out early just so you can clear out of Dodge. Or you may just want to stay around and sign up with the FBI. It looks like this might turn into a permanent assignment."

"That's just it. I'm not sure how long the FBI can stay involved in this."

Her hands flew to her hips. "Wait a minute. If this is your way of saying nice knowing you, see you around, kiddo, you have another think coming. You can't convince me I need to stay and fight a personal killer and then walk away."

He put his hands on her shoulders. "I have no intention of walking away, but if the FBI pulls out, I'll be here as a private citizen."

The words sank in slowly. "You'd no longer be Bart Cromwell, fictional man from the bureau's database of assumed identities."

"No."

"Then why would you stay? Why would you risk your life to face a killer when it's no longer your job?"

He pushed a lock of hair from her face, tucking it behind her left ear. His gaze met hers. "I know you don't want to hear this, but it's only fair I tell you. I'm crazy about you, Megan. I think I was from that first day we had lunch together and you told me off. I tried to deny it, tried to pretend the feelings weren't there, but they only grew stronger. Then last night when we kissed under the mistletoe, I had to face it. And unless I'm reading all the signals wrong, you feel something for me.''

She rested her head on his shoulder, suddenly feeling as if her legs couldn't hold her up. She felt a lot more than *something,* but she'd been determined to blame it on the pregnancy-induced hormonal imbalance. ''Has this ever happened before?'' she asked. ''I mean, when you're on a case that throws you together with a woman the way we've been thrown together, do you become emotionally attached?''

''Oh, yeah. It's almost always emotional. I usually want to kill them by the time it's over. But if you mean, do I fall the way I've fallen for you, the answer is an unequivocal no. You're the very first. And for the record, it's against every rule in the book to get hooked on the woman you're there to protect.''

He tucked a thumb under her chin and tilted her face so that her mouth was only inches from his. And then he kissed her. She felt it all the way to her toes, a sweet passion that overrode everything except her need to kiss him back.

And she did. Over and over, her mouth parting, their breaths mingling, every part of her body aching for his touch. Finally she pulled away. ''I can't make love to you, Bart. Not like this. I'm too big and too close to the due date.''

''You don't have to. I don't want to take any medical risks.''

''The doctor didn't tell me that. It's just the way I feel.''

''I've waited thirty-eight years to feel this way about a woman, Megan. I can wait a few more weeks to show you what I feel for you. But I can't wait that long to hold you and to kiss you. Not if you feel the same way I do.''

This time she kissed him, her tall, dark stranger with a gun at his side. She couldn't imagine how they'd ever fit in each other's lives, but she refused to worry about that now. Unless they found the killer soon, there wouldn't be a future to worry about.

SHE WAS STILL THINKING about Bart when she got another phone call from John. Talk about an instant comedown, she thought as she listened to tales of his latest crisis.

"Anyway, the meeting bombed. I'll be glad when your maternity leave is over and you get back on the job."

"It's nice to be missed."

"There's nothing nice about this situation. The merger team has come to a standstill in negotiations."

"I'm sure you can manage."

"Not as well as you do. I don't have the patience to deal with the details. So, when are you coming back? You have to be bored out of your mind wandering around all by yourself in that monstrosity from the Dark Ages. If you're going to stay there, you should at least update the place. Put in a lap pool and a hot tub."

"I love it at Pelican's Roost. And you know when I'm coming back. It's on your calendar."

"You can come back early."

"Don't count on it."

"Oh yeah, and your secretary said to tell you some adoption agency out of Baton Rouge called. They wanted to know if you'd made a decision yet. Surely you have this all worked out by now."

"Not exactly."

"I don't understand your dragging your feet. You're always the one after me to be more organized."

"Is that why you called my mother?"

"Don't get huffy. I just thought she could talk some

sense into you in case you're toying with the idea of keeping that baby. You said yourself that the way you live is no way to raise a child. Putting in the kind of hours we do. Traveling constantly.''

''I know what I said, John.''

''Well, not many women your age have moved up the corporate ladder as fast as you have. I'd hate to see you throw it all away out of some misplaced obligation to a child that's not even your own flesh and blood.''

''I appreciate your concern.''

''You don't sound like it. In fact, you don't sound good at all. I'm worried about you over there by yourself at a time like this. I may just drive over this weekend for a visit, take you out to dinner or something.''

''Don't bother, John. I'd hate for you to go to the trouble. Besides, I'm not by myself. A friend is staying with me.''

''Then I feel better about it. Who is she?''

''She's a he, an old college buddy.''

''Well, at least we know he's not there trying to get you into the sack. Not in the shape you're in.''

''Thank you. What a gentleman. You know just how to make a lady feel better.'' The doorbell rang. She pushed the curtain back and peeked out. It was Sandra Birney carrying a casserole dish. ''Someone's at my door, John. Is there anything business related you need to ask me?''

''I guess not. You take care. We do miss you around here, especially me. I was here until midnight putting together a report we could have done in an hour.''

A report she would have likely done without his help. ''Gotta go. Talk to you later.''

''Let us know if the baby happens to come early, which I sincerely hope it does.''

By the time she got off the phone with him, Bart was at the door greeting Sandra and introducing himself, though Megan was certain she'd already heard all about him. There were no secrets among the residents of Orange Beach.

"So YOU'RE the handsome stranger I keep hearing about."

"I hope so," Bart said, ushering the woman in the door.

"They weren't exaggerating a bit." She handed him the dish that was still warm. "I was making lasagna today, so I made extra. I don't imagine Megan feels like doing a lot of cooking."

"And even if I did, I'd still rather have your lasagna," Megan said, joining them in the living area. He watched her walk toward them, grateful to see that the phone call hadn't left her frowning.

"I'll put this in the kitchen while you two visit," Bart said. "Can I get you something, a soft drink or some water?"

"Nothing for me," Sandra said. "I'm off to the crafts fair. I just wanted to drop this off before I went, and see if Megan wanted me to pick up anything for her while I was in Fairhope."

Bart tried to think of something to entice her to stay. From the little Megan had said about her, he imagined she knew as much or more than anyone around here about what went on in Orange Beach as well as about Megan and her past. Any of which could play an important role is the danger Megan was in now.

"You have to stay at least a few minutes. Megan was just saying how much she missed having another woman to talk to."

Megan shot him an disapproving look. He smiled and ignored it.

"In that case, I can stay a few minutes. I don't really need any other dust catchers in my house anyway. And I've got enough presents under the tree to keep us opening until noon as it is."

He took the food to the kitchen, poured himself a cup of coffee and two glasses of fruit juice for the ladies. He added some cookies to the tray as well. Incentive to keep Sandra Birney talking.

They were discussing house repairs when he returned. "I see you have Mark Cox working on your house," Sandra said. "He did a few repairs for me last winter. Did a right good job at it. Reasonable, too. These big contractors charge an arm and a leg to do a little mending."

"Megan tells me you and her mother are good friends," Bart said, trying to steer the conversation back to something useful.

"We used to be. We both grew up and went to school right here. I helped her pick out the dress she wore the night she was crowned Miss Alabama."

"That must have been a very exciting event."

"I'll say. Marilyn was easily the prettiest girl in the state. She was a finalist in the Miss America pageant and a sight prettier than the girl who won if you ask me."

"Mother says the same thing," Megan agreed, "so it must be true."

"Your mother wasn't known for hiding her light under a bushel. She was a knockout and she knew it. And boy could she dance. I saw her on Broadway once. She was the best dancer in the chorus. She could have made a real name for herself if she hadn't hooked up with that Italian entrepreneur and run off to Europe."

"Was that before or after Megan was born?"

"That was way after. Megan was born the next year after she won her title. Marilyn was only nineteen when she got pregnant. Poor thing. She came to see me as soon as she realized she was late. She was scared to death. I came over here with her to tell Megan's grandmother."

"Was my grandmother upset?" Megan asked, unable to contain her curiosity.

"Oh, honey, I've never seen her that upset before or since. I won't forget that night if I live to be a hundred and fifty. Both of them crying. It was probably what kept me a virgin until the night Jeff and I married."

Bart sat his mug of coffee on the end table. "Then you must know who Megan's father is?"

Sandra stared at him as if he'd just asked for military secrets from the Pentagon. "Why would you ask that?"

Megan leaned forward. "This is important, Sandra. If you know who my father is, please tell me."

Her voice was soft, yet strained. Bart reached over and took her hand in his. He'd known that helping him sift through her life to search for a killer would be hard on her, but he hadn't realized that he was asking her to dig up a past whose secrets still had the power to hurt her.

Sandra squirmed in her chair and picked up her purse, running her fingers up and down the leather strap. "Have you asked your mother that question?"

"Many times, when I was much younger. My grandmother, too. All they would say is that it was some man Mother met while she was out of town and that we were both better off without him."

"And that's all I can tell you. I wouldn't think it would matter at this point in your life. Don't let it matter. He was never part of your life and no real part of your mother's. She's forgotten all about him and you should, too."

''But do you know his name?''

Sandra shook her head, though Bart would be willing to bet a year's pay that she was lying. And that made him all the more interested in finding out the truth. It wasn't likely that a man who'd stayed out of Megan's life for all of her thirty-one years would come back and try to kill her, but it could turn out to be a piece of the puzzle.

Sandra squirmed in her seat and ran her index finger around the rim of her juice glass. She had no doubt revealed a lot more than she'd meant to. She stood and reminded them she was on her way shopping and needed to get to the fair before all the best items were gone. By the time she made it to the door, she seemed to have recovered from her momentary plunge into nervousness and was laughing and talking to Megan about the baby.

His mind was still on Marilyn Lancaster, Miss Alabama. He walked to the picture on the piano of mother and daughter. He hated to even think what secrets that woman lived with. He was glad that the only thing Megan seemed to have inherited from her was her looks.

MEGAN OPENED the sliding doors and stared at the balcony railings that had nearly sent her plunging to her death a few nights ago. They'd been replaced, but still she had no desire to put them to the test, especially not today. The past twenty-four hours had been strange, a mixture of all that was good and all that was bad in her life.

Being with Bart had been the good part. He hadn't talked much about his feelings for her since that morning, but every touch between them had seemed to hold special meaning and every shared look had produced the sensation of a clandestine indiscretion. The beginning of intimacy, of the excitement of discovering new things about each other.

But all of that existed within the cloud of uncertainty that overrode everything they said or did. They had no idea what they were up against. At least before, it was Joshua Caraway, a devil Bart knew. Now they had no clues, and even though Bart had grilled her about every detail of her life, they had come up with no reason for anyone to want to kill her.

Only someone did.

"I shouldn't be thinking about madmen, little one. I should be reading you stories and singing you lullabies the way I did before this mess started."

Most of all, she should be talking to the adoption agency and finding the baby a home. Only she couldn't. A dozen times today she'd walked to the phone to make the call, but her fingers refused to dial the number, balked at putting in motion the procedure for giving up the baby.

She'd carried her in her womb, but another woman would be the one to cuddle her against her chest, to care for her when she was sick, to watch her take her first step and hear her say Mama for the very first time.

If the baby were going home with Jackie and Ben, giving her up might still be difficult, but she could have handled that. It would have been the right thing to do, the only choice.

And now adoption was the right thing to do. Megan wasn't parent material. She lacked nurturing skills. Work was all she knew. And she positively would not raise a child the way she had been raised, leaving her in the hands of sitters and day-care workers and anyone else who would look after her. A child needed a mother who was there.

She walked to the bed, slipped out of her shoes and stretched out on top of the quilt. Now adoption was the only answer. So why couldn't she make a simple phone call and put the final plans in motion?

Bart stepped to the door. ''I thought you might be taking an afternoon nap.''

''Just resting. I have too much on my mind to fall sleep.''

''I wish I could do something to ease the worry.''

''You do. I have my own FBI agent on full-time duty.'' She patted the bed next to her. ''Come lie down beside me.''

''If I do, I can't promise you that you'll get any rest.''

His words had grown husky, and there was no mistaking the desire that pooled in his brilliant blue eyes. ''Promises, promises. Is that all you FBI guys ever do?''

Chapter Eleven

Megan rolled onto her side to watch as Bart tugged his shirt over his head. The action left his hair mussed. By the time he stretched out on the bed beside her, her heart raced and she had the crazy feeling that she was moving in a dream, an illusion of danger and excitement far removed from her real life. And anything was possible in a dream.

She scooted closer and ran her fingers through the hairs on his chest, mesmerized by the sight of them curling around her painted nails. Her mind pictured him the way he looked that first day when he'd sauntered into the souvenir shop. Rugged, skin bronzed from the sun, hardbodied, mysterious.

His fingers tangled in her hair, and he pulled her mouth to his. The world dissolved around her as she lost herself in the sensations that coursed through her veins. Passion, arousal, excitement, craving so intense that for once she forgot the inhibitions that usually ruled her life. When they finally pulled apart she was trembling.

"Did I hurt you?" he asked.

"No. You made me feel like a woman. Hot. Alive. Seductive."

"You are all those things and more." He trailed his

fingers down her arm, then massaged the tips of her nipples through her shirt. "I've never met anyone like you."

"I can't imagine what you see in me that's different from anyone else."

"I'm not sure myself. I only know that you reach parts of me that other women don't touch, make me see myself as more than just a man with a job to do. Make me more human."

"Maybe it's just being here at Pelican's Roost that does that. It's a magical spot."

"No." He kissed her, gently this time, a quiet but almost desperate passion shining in his eyes. "I like waking up in the house and knowing you're nearby, like having breakfast with you and walking on the beach with your hand in mine. I like the sound of your voice, the way you smile when you're nervous, the way you look right now."

"I look pregnant."

"That's what you see. I see a woman who takes my breath away." He splayed his hand across her stomach. "Let me undress you, Megan."

"I don't want you to remember by body looking like this."

"But I will. I won't think of it the way you do, but I'll always remember this December and you. I meant what I said about waiting for you, but I'd like to touch you. All of you."

She sighed and looked away. She hadn't been with all that many men before, but when she had been, she'd known that her body was good, that she was attractive and had what it took to satisfy the man. But this time, she was so unsure.

He kissed the back of her neck and nibbled her earlobe. "I've seen plenty of women with great bodies, Megan, even made love to a few of them. None of them ever made me feel the way I do right now. Now, you can undress or not. It's up to you, but don't ever think that I find you less desirable because you're pregnant.''

His words stroked her like fingers of fire, and the last of her inhibitions faded into nothingness. She'd cheated death three times in the past couple weeks and still an unknown killer stalked her, waiting for a chance to finish what he'd started. She couldn't imagine a better reason to grab on to life and reach for all the gusto she could find.

She slid from the bed and started unbuttoning her shirt. The baby moved inside her, alive and kicking. Bart was lying on his side watching her, the bulge in his jeans becoming a definable shape, proof that he'd meant what he said about finding her desirable.

In the midst of danger she had a few minutes to experience a world where everything was right and she was not going to turn it down. She slid the shirt down her arms and dropped it to the floor. A few seconds later, her bra landed on top of the heap.

SUNLIGHT POURED through the doors behind Megan, casting her body in a golden glow that made her olive skin glisten and her dark hair shine as if it were wet. Bart could only watch in awe as Megan bared her full, beautiful breasts and then untied the waist of her maternity skirt and let it fall with her panties into a small mound of clothing at her feet. Provocative and sensual, she left him reeling, overwhelmed by unfamiliar feelings he couldn't fully comprehend.

Her slow, deliberate movements gave the impression that she was doing much more than baring her body. It was as if she was stripping away a protective veneer that guarded her heart and soul. It was erotic, unbelievably seductive, almost as thrilling as the act of making love itself.

His jeans became unbearably tight and binding and he stood and slipped them off, wiggling out of them and his boxer shorts as Megan threw back the coverlet and left nothing but crisp, white sheets for them to stretch out on.

He ran his hand across the flesh of her stomach. "It's hard to imagine that you have a new life inside there."

"It's a miracle. Being with you is a miracle. Feeling the way I do right now is a miracle."

She touched her fingers to his lips. "How do you feel?"

"As if my heart is tripping over itself. Like I'm weightless, and yet achy at the same time. I'm probably not saying any of this right."

"You're saying it exactly right."

She stopped the conversation with her lips on his, her tongue dipping and probing inside his mouth. And then he lost the ability to talk or think. His hands roamed her back, while she kissed him and took the hardness of him in her hands, stroking until his lungs seemed to cut off his breath.

Then she took his hand and placed it where she wanted him to touch her. Her skin was smooth as silk, and she purred as he roamed her flesh, first with his fingers, then with his lips. One second she was yielding and supple, the next she stiffened and he could feel a heated rush of moisture.

She moaned and called his name, breathing in short quick gasps before she found him again, touching, caressing, stroking, until she drove him over the top.

"Megan. Megan." Her name flew from his lips before he collapsed in a pool of slick fulfillment. He wished the moment could have lasted forever instead of just a pinpoint in time. He wished all of life could be like this. Perfect. Beautiful. A dream.

But he knew the nightmare was only a heartbeat away. Knew that one sick man could rob him and Megan of everything they'd found. But it could happen only if he slipped up. If he made a mistake. If he got too entangled in the emotions that had ridden him so hard a few seconds ago.

He couldn't let that happen. They lay there for a long time, neither of them speaking, and yet the silence wasn't awkward. It was as if they both needed time to absorb what had happened between them. Finally, he heard a gentle, rhythmic breathing and knew that Megan had fallen asleep. He was sure her body needed the rest, so he slipped his arm from beneath her and wiggled back into his jeans.

He had a killer to trap.

December 18

MEGAN ROLLED OVER in bed, sat up, and stared out the glass door and onto the beach. Apparently a front had moved in overnight. The skies were overcast and the beach was deserted again except for a few brave souls who were bundled in hats and sweatshirts.

Typical December weather for southern Alabama. Balmy days and cool nights when kids could wade in the shallow water close to land. Then a front would come through, the temperature would drop and winter would make a temporary visit to the Deep South. But the chill that had lived inside Megan for the past couple of weeks had been burned away by the fire Bart had ignited inside her. Last night she had slept in his arms.

She tried to slip out of bed and start the coffee, but he stirred the second she moved. "You are a light sleeper."

"Especially when I'm on a case. And this house makes it difficult to sleep at all. I'd swear it was haunted if I believed in ghosts."

"Don't you?"

"No. I have enough trouble with the disturbed living. I'm not about to even consider the possibility of taking on the disturbed dead. The wind here is bad enough. It screams like a crazy banshee. Listen, there it goes again."

"Legend has it," she told him, "that the wailing is the widows crying for the fishermen lovers who never came home. No one explains why they only cry when the wind is blowing. Now, why don't I go start the coffee?"

He cuddled against her, then kissed her, a long, sweet, wet kiss that made her whole body tingle. "You stay in bed, little mother-to-be. I'll get the coffee."

He came back a short while later with mugs of steaming coffee and warm, buttered slices of the bread she'd put in the bread maker last night and set to be ready by morning. A small bowl of raspberry preserves sat in the middle of the tray, along with napkins, eating utensils and glasses of fresh-squeezed orange juice.

"You are going to have me so spoiled," she said, "I won't be able to get along without you."

"That's the general idea." He pushed the clock out of the way and set the tray on the bedside table. "Actually, this is for making you relive your life in minute detail yesterday. I have a friend at the bureau running a check on about a dozen of the names you gave me. You never know what will turn up when you start searching into people's pasts."

"I can't imagine how you picked which twelve to run

background searches on. No one seemed the least bit suspicious to me.''

''It was mostly luck of the draw, but I had to start somewhere.'' He handed her a mug of coffee and took the other himself, walking to look out over the gray landscape as he sipped. ''I started with people you deal with on a regular basis, especially those you admitted were not always happy with your decisions. You wield a lot of power for a young woman. There are always people who resent that.''

''Resent? Yes. Kill me for it? Not likely.''

''There are a lot of sick people out there.''

She took a bite of the bread. She always woke up hungry these days. Before the pregnancy, she'd grab a bagel, if she bothered to eat at all. Since the pregnancy, she never missed breakfast, then snacked around ten.

''Strange, but times like this, it's hard to imagine there really is a killer. It's as if someone played a cruel hoax and now he's gone on to other things. It seems I could just go downstairs and go on with my life.''

''That's your mind's way of coping. It takes breaks from the high levels of stress and tension, keeps you from going nuts. It's kind of like the way doctors joke in the ER when they're dealing with massive injuries, or police banter at the scene of a grisly crime.''

''So what do we do today?''

''More of the same, except I'd like to have a look around in the cupola or anywhere else you think your grandmother kept souvenirs, pictures, letters—anything from the past.''

''Ooowwow!''

''Is something wrong?''

She clutched her stomach. ''The baby is active this morning. I think she's kickboxing. Put your hand right here and wait a few seconds. You'll feel her. She's a powerhouse.''

He sat on the side of the bed and put his hand over her stomach. He didn't have to wait long for the action to start. A broad grin spread across his face. ''You mean, all of that goes on in your tummy?''

''All the time. It's a veritable gym in there. If anything, it's been a little quieter of late. I'm not sure there's enough room left in there for her usual antics.''

He leaned over and kissed the spot where the baby had kicked. The act was both sweet and appealing, and her appreciation of him deepened, strengthening the bonds that fused them together. The man was totally amazing.

It was difficult to believe it had been only two weeks since they'd met, but two weeks of spending every minute together in a web of danger had a way of making the passage of time exponential, folding it over and letting years of emotions pass in the matter of days.

The sound of a car engine drifted thorough the open doors that led to the balcony.

''Don't tell me your handyman works on Sunday?''

''I wouldn't think so.''

Bart pulled on his robe as he stepped onto the balcony and walked to the corner to see who'd turned off the road and driven down to the house. Megan eased up, slid her feet into her furry slippers and wiggled into a pair of green sweatpants and matching maternity top.

''It's a cop,'' he said. ''Always around when you need them most.''

''Funny. It's probably Roger.''

''Roger?''

''Roger Collier. He's an old school friend. I called the night I arrived in Orange Beach to complain about a man who I thought might be following me.''

"Boy, think of the story he'll tell his cop buddies to-night after he finds out you let the mysterious stranger in. They'll all be kicking themselves for not following you around. Shall I get the door?"

"In your robe?" She threw up her hands in surrender. "Why not? He's probably already heard the whole story of how an old college chum drove into town, got one look at my ravishing beauty and fell madly in love with me." She flipped her hair as if she were a femme fatale and then pulled the bulky top tight around her stomach to emphasize the bulge. "I'll brush my teeth, throw some water on my face and join you two in a moment. Just don't let on that you were the guy I thought was following me."

"Me? Follow a good-looking woman I didn't know from Adam, and then just move into her house and her bed? What kind of man do you think I am?"

She made a face but left the question unanswered. She thought he was a sexy, brave superhero, exactly what she needed in her life right now. And the future was too neb-ulous at this point to think about.

BART OPENED the door, and the cop looked him over as if assessing this creature Megan had imported. There was no sign of surprise at his answering the door though, so apparently Megan was right about the rumors of her new lover reaching clear to the ears of the law.

He raked his hair back from his face. "Is there a prob-lem, Officer?"

"No. I'm a friend of Megan's. Is she around?"

"She's upstairs, but she'll be down in a minute. Would you like to come in?"

He took off his hat and worried the edges with his

fingers. "Yeah." He wiped his feet on the doormat, then stepped inside.

"Why don't you have a seat?" Bart offered, motioning to the couch. "I'll pour you a cup of coffee."

"No coffee for me. I just got off duty and I'm planning to go home and get some sleep. I could use a glass of water, though."

He followed Bart into the kitchen. "I hear you and Megan are old friends."

"News gets around fast in Orange Beach."

"We're like one big family with a heap of relatives who come in to spend the winter and another batch that comes down for the summer."

"Law enforcement must get tough during peak tourist season."

Roger rocked back on his heels, then straightened and poked out his chest. "Nothing we can't handle."

"Then you must have a fine department."

"We keep a tight lid on the town. If you're looking for trouble, Orange Beach is not the place to come."

His tough-cop image was in rare form, when Megan made it to the kitchen. "Orange Beach is one of the safest places in the country," she said, walking over to stand beside Bart. "You told me that the other night, Roger."

He stared at Bart suspiciously for a minute before switching his gaze back to her. "Have you seen any more of the man you called about?"

"Not a sign. I guess it was just the pregnancy making me a little edgier than normal."

"A big empty house on an isolated stretch of beach would make most women edgy, especially when you're here all alone."

"I guess you're right. I haven't given the man a thought since Bart arrived."

"Like I told you. Give us a call anytime you have a problem. Someone will be right out."

"So how did you get into police work?" Bart asked, not interested at all, but realizing this was a friend Megan had failed to mention yesterday when they'd been going over names of people she knew in Orange Beach. "You sound as if you enjoy it."

"I do, but I'm thinking of moving to a bigger city, someplace like Atlanta or New Orleans where there's more to police work than just stopping a few speeders and keeping drunks off the streets."

"So you'd like a little more action."

"I like getting into the head of killers, seeing how their minds work. You probably don't know this, but a lot of crimes go unsolved every year, even murders. Sometimes even when the cops know who the perpetrator is, they can't get anything on him."

Bart didn't hesitate. "Then I guess if a man's smart enough, he can get by with murder."

"If he knows the system, he can beat it. Most criminals don't. That's when we catch them."

"You take care of the killers. I'll just sell my cars."

"Where are you from?"

"Nashville. The capital of country music."

Megan had been peeling an orange while they talked. When she finished, she dropped the rind in the trash can and wiped her hands on a dishcloth. "So what did make you decide to go into law enforcement?" she asked, finally entering into the conversation. "I don't think you mentioned that you were even thinking about it when you visited me a couple of years ago in New Orleans."

"Like I told you then, I was getting over my divorce and finding myself. I visited Jackie, too. I'm glad I did, after what happened to her last month."

Megan tensed the second Jackie's name was mentioned, dropping the slice of orange she was about to put in her mouth. Bart picked it up and threw it in the trash while she regained her composure. He bent and stooped a lot more easily than she did.

"Guess I'll be on my way," Roger said. "Let you two get back to whatever it was you were doing."

"Thanks for coming by, Roger. I appreciate your checking in on me."

He lay a hand on her arm. "Glad to help. We go way back, you and me. If you need anything, even after the baby comes, just call me. But I guess you'll be going back to your job pretty soon after that."

"I'm afraid so."

Bart said his goodbye in the kitchen and watched as Megan walked Roger to the door. The guy could still have a thing for Megan. But not likely a killer. He had no real motive to want to do away with Megan. Bart would run a check on him nonetheless. As it was, they were batting zero. And it was only a matter of time before the man struck again.

His bare feet slapped across the tile kitchen floor as he poured himself another cup of coffee. It had started to rain now, and the separation between the sky and the Gulf was almost indistinguishable.

Roger Collier, a man who knew both Jackie and Megan well enough to visit them when he was going through a divorce. Maybe that was the link he needed, not necessarily Collier, but just someone who was connected with both of them. That would likely mean someone from Orange Beach, since that's where they'd become friends.

If Jackie and Megan were into something, had lent someone money they couldn't pay back or backed a business venture that went sour or...

Megan was frowning when she walked back into the kitchen. "That was not the way I'd planned to start the day, but it went okay, I thought."

"I take it Roger's an old boyfriend."

"He and Jackie went steady during most of our junior year. I dated him a few times after they broke up, but it was no big deal. He started dating a girl from Pensacola right after graduation and married her a few months later."

"The one who divorced him."

"That's the one."

"So when he visited you in New Orleans, was he trying to find a replacement for the one who got away?"

"He was trying to find a job. He wanted me to hire him. I wasn't about to fall into that trap. I got him an interview with a guy in another department. He wasn't impressed. I didn't speak with Roger again until the other day when I called the police station and he answered the phone."

"And now he decided to pay a visit."

She stretched her neck, moving it from side to side while she massaged the tendons. "Enough talk of Officer Friendly. I say we go to the cupola and see what we can find in the storage boxes and then break for an early lunch."

THEY DIDN'T MAKE IT to the cupola, but they got as far as a trunk in one of the bedrooms that held quilts and picture albums. She picked up the top one. The manila paper inside the album had turned a grayish yellow and the pictures were held in place by black tabs. About a third of the tabs had come loose, leaving the pictures hanging at odd angles. Megan recognized a couple of the snapshots as being of her grandmother when she was a girl, but mostly they were a hodgepodge of relatives who had died before she was born. Even Bart wasn't interested in going back that far.

Bart removed the other albums from the trunk, blowing away a layer of dust and piling them on the table at the edge of the bed. There were five in all.

The first three were full of black-and-white snapshots of people in long dresses and funny-looking shoes. The fourth was her childhood depicted in pictures her mother had evidently sent to her grandmother. The album was cloth-covered, but was of the newer variety, the pictures fitted nicely between slick plastic sheets.

Bart tilted the album so that it picked up more of the light from the brass and glass chandelier over the bed. "You must have been about five in this picture. There is a resemblance between you and your mother. I can see it here."

"I was four. I don't remember her taking the picture, but I've heard Grandmother say that was the house we lived in the year I was four. Mother was doing theater in Chicago then. The next year we moved to New York. We were in Brooklyn three years. That was the longest we ever lived in one place."

"That's why you're so cosmopolitan."

"Now you sound like my mother. She always found a nice way to say it, too. The problem was that no matter where we lived, she had no time for me. I always felt like an intrusion in her life. I'm sure that's why I loved it at my grandmother's. If she didn't love having me around, she certainly did a good job of pretending."

They continued turning the pages, pausing on each one. She tried to identify the men in the pictures for Bart, but they ran together in her mind. She remembered the husbands, but the boyfriends her mother had in between marriages were usually not around long enough to make a lasting impression.

"Did you and your mother argue a lot?"

"Heavens, no. We never argued. When she was around, she was all sweetness and light. She swept into a room like a vision. On the stage, she was primarily a dancer. In life, she was an actress. You know the line that says all the world's a stage? Marilyn Lancaster took it literally."

"Explain to me again. Exactly what did she tell you about your father?"

"That he was a mistake that should never have happened. When she told him she was pregnant, he deserted her and that was the end of the relationship."

"And she never told you anything else about him?"

"No. I asked a couple of times when I was younger. She got all melodramatic, doing one of her touching monologues on the fact that she had washed him from her life the way one washes away an ugly stain." Megan did her best to capture her mother's flair, but missed by a mile.

"And even as an adult you let it go at that?"

"Absolutely. One parent is more than enough. I'm really happy with my life, Bart. At least I was before my best friend died, leaving me with her unborn child growing inside me. And before a killer singled me out as his next victim."

"Then you're not going to like my next suggestion."

"Dare I ask?"

"I want you to call your mother and insist she tell you who your father is."

Chapter Twelve

It was pouring outside now, a regular deluge that ran in streams off the balconies and came down in sheets outside the kitchen window of Pelican's Roost. A fit day for the task Bart had assigned her. She was thirty-one-years old and she had never laid eyes on the man who had fathered Megan Lancaster.

The dread was so strong, it made her sick to her stomach. "You don't know what you're asking, Bart."

He stepped behind her and placed his hands on her shoulders, massaging gently. "You're right. I can't identify with having to ask your mother who your father is after three decades of not knowing. I've never been put in that position, but I can see how it's affecting you, and I'd never ask you to do it if I didn't think it was necessary."

"I don't understand why you think a man I've never seen can be connected to someone wanting me dead?"

"You don't know that you've never seen him. You can't be certain he doesn't live right here in Orange Beach, or that he hasn't been paying your mother money, or that she hasn't been blackmailing him. There are any number of possibilities."

"You've been in the crime business too long."

"Touché. But we're running out of options. I'm not trying to force you to build a relationship with this man. Once we rule out the possibility that he's involved with the attempts on your life, you can forget about him. He'll just be a name."

Only it wouldn't be that easy. Because then her father would exist. Be real. Still, she picked up the phone and punched in the number. "For you, sweetie," she said, putting a hand under her stomach. "If this helps keep you safe, it will be worth it."

With any luck, her mother wouldn't be home to answer the phone.

"Hello."

Her heart sank. "Hello, Mother."

"Megan. What a surprise."

Her mother wasn't nearly as surprised as she would be when she heard why Megan was calling. She took a deep breath and tried to decide how to phrase her question. "I was hoping I'd catch you at home. I have a question to ask."

"You just caught us," her mother said, "we were about to meet some friends for lunch and a round of golf. I hope your question is not about pregnancies or the birth process. I'm afraid all my knowledge is severely out of date."

"No. It's not about that."

"You don't sound like yourself. Is something wrong?"

Okay, here goes. "Being pregnant and giving birth has made me think about family."

"I knew something was wrong when you called." Marilyn's voice grew strained. "It's the baby, isn't it? Have they discovered some congenital birth disorder before it's even born? I hope this won't make it more difficult for her to be adopted."

"The baby's fine." She clasped the phone so hard, her fingers grew numb. "This is about me and you and my biological father. I'd like to know his name and something about him."

She heard her mother gasp and then the connection went silent. Megan's gaze fixed on the rain, the steady, rhythmic downpour, while the silence grew deafening.

"You have no father, Megan. You only have a mother. You may not like me much, but I'm it."

"I'm not trying to upset you or displace you, Mother. I told you, I feel I should know his name and a little about him, just in case I should ever need to get in touch with him. I may be having my own baby one day and he'd be part of its genetic makeup."

"Did Sandra tell you to call me about this?"

"No one told me to call you." That wasn't exactly the truth, but it fit with the rest of the lie about the reason she suddenly needed a name. "I don't plan to contact the man, Mother. At least not at any foreseeable time in the future. If nothing else, give me his name. I'm not a child any longer. You don't have to protect me from the truth."

That was it. Firm but not argumentative. If she got into a power struggle with her mother, she'd never win.

"I don't understand why you're doing this to me, Megan."

To her. That was the way her mother saw all of life. Her needs. Her wants. Her happiness. Knowing and accepting that fact gave Megan the courage to plunge ahead.

"Is he someone here in Orange Beach? Is that why you don't want to tell me his name."

"In Orange Beach? Whatever gave you that idea?"

"I'm only asking."

"Fine, if this is the way you want it."

"It is."

"I can give you his name. That's all I know. I have no idea where he lives or even what he does. He could be married with six kids or possibly dead."

"I understand," she said flatly.

"There was never a real relationship between the two of us. I met him on that study trip to Paris the year after I was named Miss Alabama. He was impressed with my title and I was infatuated because he was French and handsome. That's all it ever was."

"I'm not asking for details, Mother. And I'm not judging you. I only want to know his name and any information you can give me about where he lives."

"As far as I know, he still lives in Paris. His name is Franois Grauvier."

"Can you spell that?"

Megan printed the name as her mother spelled. "Is he about your age?"

"He's older, much older. At least ten years."

"Thank you, Mother. I know you find it difficult to talk about this man, but I appreciate your sharing the information with me."

"I understand fully. He's a nonidentity to me, but if you want to know about him, there's no reason for me not to tell you."

The change in her voice was dramatic. It was as if releasing the information about his identity destroyed some of the demons her mother had nursed for three decades. They chatted a few minutes more, *attempted* small talk anyway, then ended the conversation with her mother telling her she wanted to know as soon as the baby was born.

Megan breathed a sigh of pure relief as she broke the connection. It had not been as traumatic as she'd expected. The man lived in France. There was no reason why their paths would have to cross. She hadn't had a father for the first thirty-one years of her life. She definitely didn't need one now.

"I have the name, Bart, but you can cross my biological father off your list. He's a Frenchman. She met him on a trip to Paris and hasn't heard from him since."

The good news, however, was also bad. They'd hit another dead end.

MARILYN LANCASTER'S HANDS trembled as she placed the phone back in its cradle. No one had to tell her that she'd lacked nurturing genes. She'd tried, but mothering had never worked for her. It wasn't that she didn't love Megan. She did. In her own way. Besides, Megan was so independent, she didn't need a mother who smothered her and insisted on sharing every detail of her life.

Still, she began the downward spiral into one of her blue slumps. This was the first time she'd openly lied to Megan. If there had been any other way, she wouldn't have lied now, but some secrets had to be carried to the grave. Perhaps it didn't matter anymore. The graves were almost full. But she'd made a bargain, and it was too late to go back on it now. For her sake and for Megan's.

Opening the cabinet door, she found the container of tranquilizers and twisted it open. Tilting it, she dropped one tablet into her hand, then slipped it between her lips as old memories haunted her mind like a demon possessed.

Even now just the thought of the man reopened the wounds, released the bitter taste of betrayal. Some things never changed.

A CLAP OF THUNDER shook the house like an earthquake, startling Megan from a state somewhere between sleep and never-never land. She opened her eyes and stared out the huge wall of glass at a landscape that had passed dreary and oppressive about two inches of rain ago.

She rubbed the heels of her hands across her eyes. "I must have fallen asleep."

"You did, about an hour ago."

"You should have wakened me."

"I figured you needed the rest."

"I seem to always need rest these days. I managed easily on six hours of sleep a night before I got pregnant. When I return to work next month, I'll have so much to catch up on, I'll be lucky if I get that." She stretched, rolling her shoulders, then massaging the small of her back with her fingertips. "I think I'll make some hot tea. We can take it with us up to the cupola, or better yet, I'll take the electric pot and we can brew it up there."

"Are you sure you feel like climbing two flights of steps?"

"As long as I take it slow and easy. I can't race you to the top the way I used to do Jackie."

She gathered the items for tea, put them on a wicker tray and gave them to Bart. His balance was far better than hers at this point. The cupola was on the roof, and though the steps to reach it were on the inside, the staircase was much narrower than the others in the house. It was darker, too, especially on days like this when the sun was hidden behind layers of dingy rain clouds.

When she was very young and not allowed to climb the steep steps, she imagined they led to a tower where ghosts lived, and that if she was very bad, her mother would lock up there with them. She wasn't sure where she'd gotten such an idea except that when the door at the top of the stairs was left open, the staircase was cooler than any other spot in the house.

Strange, but she had the same feeling today. Only the ghosts they were looking for wouldn't be eerie figures clad in white. They'd be specters in pictures, or letters. But would they offer some indication that there were secrets that motivated a madman to want to take her life?

Her breathing was labored, her footsteps slow by the time they reached the door to the cupola, not so much from the climb as from the fear. It had begun its familiar slow march, walking across her flesh before chilling her inside so that she longed to crawl under a woolen blanket.

Grisly images merged in her mind. Jackie's body blown to pieces. Herself fighting for air beneath a pounding, rolling body of water. Deadly falls and gunshots in the darkness.

And sometimes, in the middle of the night, the image was a dead baby. And that was the worst of all.

"You're pale, and shaking." Bart wrapped his arms around her and held her close. "I hate that I'm having to put you through this."

"It's not your doing. You're only trying to help."

"Then I hate the fact that it's taking so long." He rested his chin on the top of her head. "We're going to win, Megan."

"I know. Most of the time, I can deal with it. Only every now and then, I feel as if we're puppets and that the killer has all the controls."

"He doesn't. We'll stop him one way or another, but this would be easier if we knew who he was. That's why we have to keep going over every aspect of your life. If we find a motive, we'll have our man. Money and love are the two most common motivations, or, more to the point, greed and rejection."

"I have a substantial amount of savings and a retirement fund. Nothing anyone would kill for."

"And you have this house. Pelican's Roost and the land it sits on is probably worth close to half a million dollars."

"It was appraised at four hundred thousand. That's nothing in today's real estate market." She turned the knob, pushed the door open and stepped into the small room.

Bart followed, a step behind. "Was your mother upset that your grandmother left the house to you and not to her?"

"Heavens, no. She hates this place. When she came home for a visit, she couldn't wait to leave."

"She might have wanted it for the selling price."

"My grandmother left her some cash. Besides, I think she probably gave Mother a little financial support through the years. Looking back, I know there were long periods of time when Mother didn't have work, and I don't remember money being a problem."

"Were you rich?"

"Not rich, but there was always enough. Even in college, Mother managed to pay my tuition and send me spending money every month. Of course, she seldom went long without having a man in the picture, and she was never attracted to poor suitors."

"And there's no other relative who thought the house should be left to them?"

"No other relatives at all." She leaned against the doorframe. "I think you can rule out greed, Bart. I don't have anything valuable enough to kill for."

"If we rule out greed, that leads us to rejection."

"There is definitely no stream of broken hearts in my past. As a matter of fact, I don't even remember one."

"I wouldn't be too sure about John Hardison. The two

of you were engaged, practically at the altar before you broke it off.''

"He probably suffered all of ten minutes before he found a new girlfriend.''

"How did the two of you come to be working so closely together?''

"He was working on a major merger, and when the work got too much for him to do by himself, he was authorized to hire another administrative person for his department. He recommended me for the position. It amounted to a nice promotion.'' She saw the look in his eye and knew what he was thinking, but he was wrong. "John recommended me because he knows I'm capable and a workaholic. Besides, we have different skills that compliment each other in this kind of job.''

"Does he ever give any indication that he'd like for the two of you to be an item again?''

She shook her head. ''Not that he wouldn't sleep with me again if I'd go along with it. He's let me know as much when we're out of town together, but he doesn't push the issue.''

Bart nodded, but let the conversation drop. She watched as he circled the stacks of boxes. The cupola was round, about twelve feet in diameter with six large windows and a narrow door that led out to the widow's walk. Boxes lined the walls, stacked three high, blocking most of the light that would have filtered through the windows. The light fixture was a one-hundred-watt bulb hanging from the center of the room.

He slapped his hand across the top of one of the boxes. "Eenie-meanie-miney-mo. Pick a box and then let's go. Care to make the first choice?''

"The task looks daunting.''

"But we could find what we're looking for in the first

box. I think we should try this one." He pulled a packing box from the stack and set it in the center of the room.

She read the identifying label, printed with a black magic marker: MEGAN'S HIGH SCHOOL YEARS IN ORANGE BEACH. "That's probably yearbooks, class pictures, my old cheerleading uniform, dried corsages from the proms and various other items of little interest."

"You never know." He took out his pocketknife and sliced through the tape. Right on the top was an eight-by-ten glossy of her and Jackie in their senior-prom dresses. Bart picked it up and studied it. "You almost look like sisters."

She stared at the picture for a minute, then let it drop through her fingers. Jackie should be here now. They should be looking at the pictures together, laughing and talking about the baby that was about to be born. Tears stung her eyes. "I can't do this, Bart. I just can't do this."

Bart jumped to his feet and took her hands in his. "Look, it's stopped raining. Let's step outside and get a breath of fresh air."

He opened the door and a gust of wind hit them in the face. She stepped though the door, started to take hold of the balustrade, but thought better of it, staying close to the wall instead. The widow's walk was narrow, no more than two feet in width, but it circled the entire cupola. Only one level higher than her bedroom, but the view had always seemed vastly different from up here.

Probably because it seemed as if she was walking the edge, looking down from a more precarious position. That and the fact that the railing was lower. A person could easily lean over too far and topple to their death. It was no place for the young, the frail or the feeble.

"I don't think I'd like to stand out here in a hurricane,"

Bart said, walking around and shaking the wooden balustrade to make certain it was tight and secure.

"No, but it's a great place to sail paper airplanes from or to blow bubbles. That's what we did the first time my grandmother brought me up here. I wasn't allowed up here by myself until I was in the seventh grade and then I was cautioned that I should never stand too close to the railing."

"Too bad we didn't bring paper. I make a mean glider."

"I'll bet you do."

"Did you ever make love in the cupola?"

"Now, wouldn't you like to know."

"You did. I can tell by that smile. Was Roger the lucky boy?"

"Pleeease!" She knew what he was doing, teasing her out of the flash of depression that had hit when she'd seen the picture of Jackie and herself. It was working. Already she felt lighter, more ready to face the facts head-on and deal with whatever she had to in order to put this ordeal behind her.

Only, there was one matter she had to clarify first, a feeling she had. "You haven't quite given up the idea that the attempts on my life are still tied to the explosion and to Jackie, have you?"

"Not entirely."

"But your boss apparently thinks this has nothing to do with Joshua Caraway."

"We've disagreed before. A case looks different in the office than it does in the field. Even if the attempts on your life are not related to Ben's testimony against Caraway, it could have something to do with you and Jackie. She's killed in an explosion. A month later someone comes after you. The timing is too bizarre, especially with you carrying her baby.''

"I loved her like a sister, Bart. She's the only really close friend I've ever had, but there's nothing there that would give rise to your theory.''

"Maybe you just haven't remembered the right thing yet.''

"There's nothing to remember. No loans. No business ventures. No love triangles. No deep dark secrets from our pasts. Nothing.'' She moved to the balcony, unafraid now that she'd seen Bart check it all out.

He stepped behind her, circled her waist with his arms and put his mouth to her ear. "If I had lived in Orange Beach when you did, I'd have hoped you'd have a few deep dark secrets and that I was part of them.''

"You're here now.'' She turned around and locked her arms around his neck. She stretched to tiptoe and touched her lips to his. A temporary reprieve that in the end might only add more complex decisions to her life. She couldn't imagine forever with him, had never been able to imagine forever with any man. But she needed him now.

He held her close as the wind whipped through her cotton shirt and blew her hair into her face. Hurling paper airplanes and watching soap bubbles float out to sea had never been as thrilling as standing on the deck of the cupola in Bart Cromwell's arms.

MEGAN STRETCHED and pushed her sleeve back to catch a glimpse of her watch. They had been at this for three hours and she was tired to the bone. Weary of going through endless boxes and coming up with things like a white shoe-polish handprint on red paper that she'd given her grandmother the Valentine's Day she was five and an old newspaper with an ad for a twenty-two-cent loaf of bread. The fatigue had lulled her into a state of adolescent silliness.

She pulled out an ad for a swimsuit that bared nothing and broke into giggles again. "Can't you just visualize this in a special swimsuit edition of *Sports Illustrated?* Bambi bears all—clear up to her kneecaps."

Bart pulled the next box from the stack. "I've never seen you so giggly. Are you sure you didn't sneak a spot of liquor into that last cup of tea?"

"Nope, bad for the baby. Some people get cranky when they get tired. I get silly. You should see me at one of the department's late-night strategy meetings. I'm a barrel of laughs."

"Not me. I'd be the old crank in the corner nodding off."

"You could never be a crank. You're a teddy bear."

"A teddy bear, am I? I'll show you teddy bear." He flexed a few muscles, then grabbed a new box from the stack, threw it to the floor with a vengeance and pointed at it with the blade of his pocketknife. "Nobody calls Agent Bart Cromwell a teddy bear and lives to tell about it."

She broke into giggles again.

He shook his head and cut the tape that bound the box. This one wasn't labeled, but it appeared to be full of old clothes. He lifted the first item and held it up for her inspection. It was a soldier's uniform, probably from her grandfather's tour of duty in WWII.

Bart slipped his arms into the jacket. "I like it. Does a man in uniform do anything for you?"

"Probably not as much as one *out* of uniform."

"Get your mind out of the gutter, lady, before I have to take care of you."

"Promises. Promises."

"I'll show you about promises later." He shrugged out of the jacket and pulled out a plaid French beret, giving it a good shake before plopping it on his head. "*Voilà, mademoiselle*, this is for you."

"*Merci, monsieur*." She mimicked his fake French accent and took a large-brimmed, flower-trimmed hat from his extended hand. The flowers were faded and crushed and the few inches of net veiling was puckered and torn. Still, she perched it on her head at a cocky angle.

"Do you have plans for the night, soldier boy? If not, I can show you a real good time."

"Sorry. I'm here with a giggly pregnant woman. Give me your number, and I'll call you later."

She gave him a playful punch to the arm. "What else is in there?" Deciding to search for herself, she bent over the box and began rummaging through the contents. Tugging on a scrap of red silk, she pulled out a party dress, floor-length with a border of lace around the neckline, low enough to give a mere glimpse of cleavage.

"I'll bet your grandfather picked that out."

"No doubt. I was sorry I never got to know him. Grandmother's eyes always sparkled when she talked about him. I know they were very much in love."

"The way it should be between a married couple."

"I agree." She dug deeper, looking for something that interested her. She'd given up on finding any item that would make a difference in Bart's investigation. "Oh my goodness. Would you look at this?"

Bart helped her free the yards of material. "A wedding dress."

"It's my grandmother's. I've seen pictures of her wearing it. I wish I'd known it was up here. I would have rescued it long ago."

Holding it up in front of her, she took a few steps, letting the fabric swish against her ankles.

She stopped when she noticed the way Bart was looking at her, rapt, as if he were seeing her for the very first time.

"You look like a vision, all white and lacy and pure."

His voice had taken on a husky quality that made her uncomfortable, made her feel as if he was seeing something in her that wasn't there. As if the dress had cast a spell on him.

"I don't think this dress was designed for a woman eight and a half months pregnant," she said, keeping her own voice light, determined to defuse the moment. "I'd have to find someone to walk in front of me and hide the bulge with the train."

"Pregnant or not, you'd make a beautiful bride."

"Now who's been slipping bourbon into the tea?" She dropped the dress back into the box, then pulled her hat from her head and threw it on top. She clasped her hands under her stomach. "Time for us to persuade Bart to give it up for the night, little one. You and I have had enough fun for one day."

Bart's expression didn't change, and the electricity that sparked the air between them grew oppressively thick. "Have you thought about keeping the baby?"

The question hit her with the force of a brick hurled at close range. "Where did that come from?"

"It's been on my mind. I know it's none of my business, but you seem so attached to the baby and you'd make a wonderful mother."

"A wonderful mother? How would I know how to do that?" Something dark and onerous swelled inside her, and she turned away from him before he read the torment in her eyes.

"You're not your mother, Megan."

"I know that. I'm me, but that's no better, not when it comes to being a wife or a mother."

He stepped in front of her and took her hands in his. "That's a cop-out statement, and you know it."

"I can't keep this baby. My job is too demanding. I travel all the time. I don't nurture. I don't even know how."

A cruel shudder shook her body as the truth hit her with shock waves of reality. She wanted this baby more than she'd ever wanted anything in her life. Giving it up was going to be as painful as having her heart ripped from her body. And yet she was afraid to keep it, afraid she'd fail it, afraid that she'd be no better than her mother.

"I'm sorry, Megan. What you do with the baby is none of my business."

"You're right. It isn't. You do what you want to, Bart. I'm going back downstairs now."

"I'll go with you. I don't like you maneuvering these stairs alone."

He took her arm as they started down the staircase. Neither of them mentioned Jackie or the baby again, except the feelings of regret and remorse pricked at her heart like rusty needles.

But she'd get used to the pain, get used to the fact that she would never hold and love the baby that grew inside her. The same way she'd gotten used to knowing that her mother would never be the kind of mother other girls had. Never be there to talk over her problems or listen to her fears.

She'd do what she had to do, and that meant placing a call to an adoption agency, this time completing the arrangements to give the baby away.

BART STARED at the screen of his laptop, a series of columns and rows and figures and data. He'd made a fire for Megan then spent the last hour manipulating information, and he was no closer to having any ideas about the identity of their mystery killer.

Maybe there was no killer out for Megan. Perhaps some guy had just been walking alone on the beach the other night when he cracked, kind of like a sniper who just goes into a business and starts shooting. Only this man reacted to a pregnant woman alone, in the dark, standing at the water's edge.

And as for the railing, it could have just become worn and looked as if it had been cut. And all of that had just happened to come a month after the mother of the baby Megan was carrying had been killed in an explosion that as yet no one had explained to his satisfaction.

And maybe Santa Claus really had magical reindeer who flew around the world every year in one night so that he could deliver toys built by little elves at the North Pole.

There was a killer and he would return. That was basically the only thing he was sure of anymore. That and the fact that he was falling hard for Megan Lancaster, though he wasn't sure he understood her at all. Every instinct he had told him that Megan was dying inside at the prospect of giving away the baby, and yet she was determined not to keep it.

She was the smartest, most successful, most together woman he'd ever known, yet she still had a perception of herself that didn't gel with the facts. He wasn't a shrink. He understood a lot more about crime than he did about women, but he knew that Megan could be one hell of a mother if that was what she wanted.

And any man would be damn lucky to have her for a wife.

The ringing of his cell phone broke into his thoughts. He grabbed it and took the call. Luke Powell identified himself and jumped right into his news.

"We finished running the check on about half of those names you gave us. Mark Cox has a couple of DWI's on his record and one arrest for possession of a controlled substance. All more than three years ago. What's his connection to Megan?"

"No real connection. He's doing some work on her beach house and I wanted to know his background."

"Then you can probably check him off the suspect list. The only thing that showed up on the other names you gave us were a few traffic violations and one teenage shoplifting record."

"So why are you working on a Sunday night? Is there something big in the works."

"No. Beth's out of town and the house got lonely. The weather's too lousy for doing much of anything but work, so I drove down to the office."

"Same here. It's been raining since morning, but I'm glad to get the results, even if they don't help."

"It's not all a loss. I have word from the lab that's examining the material from the scene of the explosion."

More news, and this time Bart prayed it would be something positive, something that would tie the explosion to Megan and provide at least a trace of a clue as to who was behind the violence.

"Hit me with it."

Chapter Thirteen

Bart broke the connection and went to find Megan, aggravation scraping along his nerve endings like fingernails against an open wound. All he asked for was one lousy break, but every door he managed to crack open slammed right back in his face.

He found Megan in the family room thumbing through a copy of *Newsweek*. She looked up when he walked in, and his heart plunged. She'd obviously taken a shower while he worked. Hair damp and pulled back, face freshly scrubbed, but still the complexities and danger she lived with shadowed her dark eyes and tugged her lips downward.

"I thought we'd have a cup of soup by the fire," she said, turning to stare at the crackling blaze.

"Sounds good to me." He walked over, turned his back to the flames and put his hands behind him to catch the heat. "I'll even warm the soup."

"It's already simmering. You know me. I can't go too long without eating."

"That's because you're eating for two."

"And I'm taking advantage of that excuse to the very end."

She snuggled farther under her throw, but at least she was smiling—for now anyway. He slipped his fingers into the back pocket of his jeans, staying in his position by the fire. "I had a call from my supervisor a few minutes ago."

"On Sunday night. Does this mean bad news?"

"Yes and no. I told you that the FBI lab was checking out some materials found at the explosion site."

She narrowed her eyes, and her lips drew into thin lines that all but disappeared. "Did they find something?"

"The report was inconclusive."

"Wouldn't that mean that this was just a freak accident, the way the local authorities believed in the beginning?"

"No, it only means that if it was a bomb, it was strategically placed and strong enough that it destroyed the evidence."

"I'm almost glad we don't know for certain. It's easier for me to accept that Jackie was killed in a freak accident that was no one's fault than to believe she was deliberately murdered. Besides, even if Joshua Caraway was behind the explosion, he can't be behind the attempts on my life. He was in jail for the last one, so knowing that the explosion was planned wouldn't help us find the man who tried to kill me."

He should let it go at that for now, but he couldn't. The stakes were too high, and even though what he had to say was not going to set well with Megan, he had to plod ahead. "I'm not ready to rule out the possibility that the explosion and the attacks on your life are not related."

"I've thought about this, too, Bart. Constantly. There's not a shred of evidence to support that claim. Even your supervisor must think that or he wouldn't be ready to close the case and pull the FBI out of this."

He met her gaze, knew she wanted precise, definite answers, but he couldn't give them to her. Solving crimes wasn't like attacking problems in the business world. There was no bottom line, no company policy or union negotiations. It was as much instinct and hunches as it was facts.

"What is it you want from me, Bart? I've told you every detail of my life."

"I need to know about Jackie."

"She was the sweetest person you'd ever want to meet. Everyone who knew her admired her not only for her disposition but for the way she tackled her complications from diabetes without complaining. She had no enemies."

"You admit that the two of you had almost lost touch over the past few years. Something might have been going on that you didn't know about."

"We'd talked at least once a week since I'd agreed to carry their child."

"But the years before that, before Ben. Did you ever hear her mention a lover who might still be bitter over her marrying Ben?"

"They'd been married for three years. No one carries a grudge that long."

"You'd be surprised." He wouldn't go into that, wouldn't drag her through the horror stories of sick men and women who nursed grudges for years until one day they finally lost it. The results were sometimes too gruesome for words. He'd seen it all. Still, given enough time, most men and women survived broken relationships and even marriages with their mental functions intact.

He had—more or less. Now, here he was falling again, this time for a woman who seemed more afraid of commitment than he'd ever been. So afraid, she was about to give up a baby, even though he was convinced it wasn't what she wanted.

"What about an affair? Did Jackie ever mention anyone, maybe someone she worked with who she was attracted to. Would she have told you if she'd strayed?"

Megan slid her legs to the floor and stuffed her feet into a pair of fluffy slippers. "She was in love with Ben from almost their first date. He was all she talked about. Him and the houseful of children she wanted. As it turned out, she was going to settle for one."

"And she has no remaining family?"

"None that I know of. If she had relatives, they weren't close enough that any of them showed up at the funeral. Certainly no one who's stepped forward and offered to take her child when it's born."

Megan was right. There was no reason to think this could be about Jackie and her baby, and yet he couldn't quite let it go. Probably because if he did, he had nothing at all to hang an investigation on.

But if Jackie was the target of the explosion, then the person who killed her could have found out about the baby the same way he had. An idle remark from one of the neighbors. A break-in at Jackie's doctor's office, taking drugs to make it look as if that was the purpose of the burglary.

Or it could have been all coincidence. His being here could be the result of a quirky turn of fate.

Grabbing the poker, he took his frustration out on the pile of logs, punching and rearranging them until they erupted in hot flames that licked their way up the chimney. The answers were out there. He just had to find them. Quickly. Before the would-be killer struck again.

He'd promised Megan he could keep her safe, but the odds were building in favor of the madman.

December 19

MONDAY MORNING BROUGHT an end to the rain, but not to the overcast skies and cooler temperatures. Megan was complaining of a backache. He was glad she saw the doctor again tomorrow.

Even in the short time he'd been here, he could tell she was tiring more easily, though she still had more mental energy than any woman he'd ever met. She'd been on the phone an hour this morning, dictating letters to her secretary and she was at her laptop now typing away.

He was pacing and trying to stay out of Fenelda Shelby's way as she worked her way from room to room with her dust cloth and basket of cleaning supplies in hand. Mark was outside, repairing some rotten boards under the eaves before he started painting. The whir of a vacuum cleaner on the inside, the sounds of pounding on the outside and the clicking of keys upstairs.

Everyone hard at work on a task they could accomplish. He envied them. Here he was wading through the same mud, sinking deeper and deeper and getting no closer to solid ground. Two women, bound by friendship and an unborn baby. One was dead. The other had survived three attempts on her life in a matter of two weeks.

But what was the motive? Inheritance? There was no one around to inherit from. A business deal gone bad? No business deals. A kinky three-way romance? No way. An old grudge? No sign of one.

But there had to be a motive. Either he hadn't hit on the right scenario yet or the facts had been manipulated. Someone either knew something they weren't telling or else someone had deliberately lied to obscure the truth.

He walked to the kitchen, poured a cup of coffee and joined Fenelda in the family room where she was polishing furniture and cleaning glass. "You swing a mean dust cloth, Mrs. Shelby. I would have thought it would take a week to clean a house this big, and you have the place starting to shine after a couple of hours."

"Land sakes, boy, as long as I've been cleaning houses for people in Orange Beach, I should be fast. I don't do any of the rental condos, though. Tourists are too messy when they're staying on the beach, but a family in their own house, that's different. Still, I'm choosy. Mrs. Lancaster was a jewel to work for and Megan's even easier. This is the longest she's been here at one time since her grandmother died."

"I take it you've lived in Orange Beach all your life."

"I moved here with my husband and son the year Leroy was four years old," she said, still pushing the cloth around the top of the coffee table. "He's twenty-eight now. I've seen some changes. I'll tell you that. Seen condos spring up like mushrooms in a field after a few days' rain. Seen people with a chunk of waterfront property go from poor to rich in the time it takes me to cook a pot of stew."

"Then you must have known Jackie Brewster."

"I did. Only I knew her as Jackie Sellers. I was some upset when I heard about her getting killed like that. You just never know. I'm glad her parents weren't still alive to have to deal with it. She was her mother's life, all Janelle Sellers could talk about."

"I heard they were close."

"The closest. I knew them all, you know, the whole Sellers family. Jackie's dad was a nice guy, kind of quiet. A looker he was, too. That's probably why Janelle kept such a close watch over him. Janelle could be nice, but she was moody. You didn't want to get on her bad side."

"Janelle Sellers and her husband must have both been only children."

"What makes you think that?"

"Megan said there was no family at Jackie's funeral. Usually, even if a person's parents are dead, they have aunts, uncles, cousins, somebody close enough to come to the funeral."

"I don't know much about Janelle. She's from some small town, up in Ohio I think. But Lane Sellers had family, at least he had a sister-in-law and a nephew, so I'm guessing he had a brother somewhere, though I never saw him. I think he ran out on his family. Anyway, the sister-in-law lived back there off Canal Road for a while. They moved away years ago. I don't even remember their names. Lane grew up right here in Orange Beach. He knew everybody in town."

"I heard he was raised by his dad."

"I never heard that, but it sounds reasonable. I do know that Janelle got something stuck in her craw about her father-in-law and she never let him in her house again."

"Did she ever say what he did?"

"Said he was a rotten traitor, but never anything more specific than that. I think he took her husband's side against hers, but that was years ago, right after I moved here. I wasn't even cleaning houses back then. I just heard her mention it every now and again after the fact. That woman could be vindictive when she took a notion. I never wanted to get on her bad side."

Fenelda kept talking, covering dozens of people he'd never heard about, but nothing seemed to fit the missing link he was searching for. He excused himself and walked outside. Even with gray skies, there was something calming about watching the waves roll to shore. What he needed was some new fact to roll in on one of them. Any clue would do.

MEGAN SCRIBBLED more notes in her notebook. She'd been working fast and furiously ever since she'd crawled out of bed that morning, burying herself in a frenzy of office-related work. A few times her subconscious had interrupted the furor to remind her that there was no escape from her feelings, but she'd quickly hushed it with another spreadsheet or financial report.

Now her fingers were growing tired, her mind weary, and she was succumbing to the onslaught of emotions that were tormenting her with increasing frequency these days. Images filled her mind—rocking a beautiful baby girl, feeding her, dressing her. Only sometimes the baby was a toddler and they were walking hand in hand on the beach, discovering brightly colored shells and letting the cool water lap at their feet.

The ache swelled inside her, overpowering as always. There was no denying it anymore. Yet how could she keep the tiny baby girl growing inside her?

Her job had become her world, the only place she'd ever truly belonged besides Pelican's Roost. She was needed there, valued. But the job was demanding and time-consuming and required extensive travel. She had nothing to offer a baby. She'd be the same kind of failure as a parent that her mother had been.

Her hands shook and the pen slipped through her fingers and bounced off the notebook and onto the table. Women had babies all the time and they didn't go to pieces the way she was doing just thinking about the possibility. What was wrong with her that she was too afraid to try? The same way she'd been too afraid to try marriage, walking out on the wedding to John the day before the invitations were supposed to go in the mail. She took a deep breath and clasped her hands in her lap to hide the trembling as she heard Bart's footsteps coming down the hall.

"Are you going to run that company from your hospital bed?"

"I don't run the company," she answered.

"Couldn't prove it by the zeal you've exhibited this morning."

"There's no reason not to work. Fenelda has the house under control."

"We could take a drive up the beach."

"Is that what you want to do?"

The doorbell rang and Bart reacted on impulse. She could see his muscles tighten, his facial features sharpen, his hand touch his gun. A few seconds later, they heard Fenelda talking to her son.

The voices carried clearly up the staircase, as did the inflections.

"I told you not to come over here bothering me today. I don't have any money to give you." Fenelda's tone was clipped, tinged with anger.

"I'll pay you back."

"With what? You don't have a job and you've made no effort to find one."

"You never cut me any slack. I told you I've got a deal in the making. Before long, I'll have all the money I need. All I'm asking for is a loan. Either I get it from you or I get it any way I can."

"Don't threaten me, Leroy. I've done and done and done for you and it's always the same. I know why you want the money, and I'm not paying for the habit, not paying to watch you kill yourself looking for a high."

"I'm out of here."

"No, Leroy, wait. I'll give you a little, but I can't spare

much. The insurance is due and I've got your hospital bills to pay.''

''Fine. Keep your money. I don't need it bad enough to beg anyway.'' The door slammed, and Megan could hear the loud clumping of his shoes as he ran down the flight of stairs to ground level. And she could hear the muffled sound of Fenelda crying.

Bart walked out to the balcony and she went down the steps to console the housekeeper who'd long ago become a family friend. Motherhood apparently did not come easy for Fenelda Shelby and she was a kind, loving woman who'd been home every night. But at one time, she'd carried Leroy inside her womb just as Megan did Jackie's baby. At one time, she must have had dreams and visions and hopes for his future. And even now, she must love him through her tears. Motherhood didn't come with guarantees.

BART WALKED to the corner of the balcony, not stopping until he had a view of Leroy Shelby stomping down the stairs. The guy was headed for trouble, and from the sound of things, he'd already had a good sampling of it. If he kept on this track, he'd wind up in jail or dead. When this was over, Bart would offer to talk to him, though he didn't have a lot of faith it would help. The young man was wallowing in self-pity and seething with anger. A recipe for grief.

Leroy walked over and stopped under the ladder where Mark Cox was working. He yelled a greeting, and the handyman climbed down. They appeared to be about the same age, though Mark was a good thirty pounds heavier, muscled where Leroy was scrawny. Tanned where Leroy's flesh was a pasty white from spending too much time inside.

He couldn't hear what they were saying. Leroy was speaking a lot softer now and the words were blotted out by the pounding of the surf. Mark pulled out his wallet and handed something to Leroy. Bart couldn't see what, but he suspected it was a few bills. He'd said he'd get money one way or another. Begging was a lot safer than other ways Bart could think of, but if the guy was on drugs, he'd eventually resort to more severe means.

Or maybe he had already. Damn. He'd be just the kind of guy Joshua Caraway would recruit if he was looking for someone to do the dirty work for him. It could happen in spite of what Luke had said about Caraway doing his own killing. The man had spent eight years in jail. He might have been determined to stay out of the limelight and out of jail. If so, he'd failed.

But Leroy would have been the perfect choice, and Joshua could have easily found out about him through underworld drug circles. Other things fit as well. Leroy had access to the house. He could have easily cut the railing and fit it back into place so that it would give when Megan put her weight against it, could have done it the day they came home and found him outside waiting to get in and fix the plumbing. Could have even done it before Megan arrived in Orange Beach.

That would also explain the money he said he was going to have coming in. He'd get it when the job was completed successfully. It was a long shot, but he'd get a tail on him immediately.

A long shot was better than no shot, and he'd been playing that game for weeks.

"I'M GLAD you suggested we get out of the house for a while," Megan said, stopping to look at a collection of porcelain angels.

"I didn't suggest we go shopping."

"Give me a break, Bart. One more day of being up cooped up inside the house and I was going to go stir-crazy. Besides, this store is so small, you can practically touch me from any spot in the place. So try to catch the spirit while I pick up a few gifts."

His gaze scanned the area before coming back to settle on her. "What are you looking for?"

"I don't know. What does a woman get a big, tough FBI agent for Christmas? Oops!" She looked around quickly, realizing that no one else in town knew he was FBI. Fortunately no one was in eavesdropping distance. "What does a sexy, good-looking car salesman like you want from Santa?"

He leaned in close and put his mouth to her ear. "A sassy, pregnant woman makes a unique gift."

"I may not be pregnant by Christmas."

"In that case I'd have to settle for a has-been."

"Not pregnant. I almost can't remember what that was like."

"You'll get a refresher course in a few days."

"Eight more if the baby's on time."

"Finish your shopping," he said. "But make it quick."

"Relax. You're the only man in the store." She rounded a bin of seasonal books and stopped to browse. She picked up a couple, read the back-cover blurbs, then slipped them back into place.

Her attention was drawn to one with a picture of a young woman holding a baby in front of a beautifully decorated Christmas tree. The baby's eyes were wide with wonder and one pudgy hand was reaching toward a shiny red ornament. She lay her hand against the cover, her fingers moving across the slick surface, while an undefined need ripped through her senses.

She pushed the book aside and turned away, backing into a pair of strong arms.

"Easy does it."

She turned and stared into a pair of steely gray eyes. Roger Collier in his police uniform. "I didn't know you were standing there," she said.

"So that's why you nearly knocked me down."

"That and the fact that I'm the size of a linebacker." She looked around but didn't see Bart.

"If you're looking for your boyfriend, he's a few feet behind you, eyeing us like a mean watchdog. I guess he'll be here for Christmas."

"I'm not sure."

His eyebrows rose into tiny fringed arches. "You two aren't having trouble, are you?"

"No. Everything's fine."

Strange, but the fact seemed to irritate him. He shuffled his feet and rested the heel of his right hand on the butt of his gun.

"I don't guess you've had any more trouble out at Pelican's Roost."

"Not a bit." She had her cover lines down pat.

"That's good to hear. But you be careful wandering around that big old house in your condition. All those stairs. All those balconies. It wouldn't take much to produce a dangerous fall."

He sounded almost sinister, but it was probably only her reaction to his words that made it seem that way. Playing hopscotch with a killer could do that to you.

"I'll be fine." The words were spoken with an assurance she didn't feel.

"I hope so. I'd be careful who I let hang around out there with me if I were you."

"Are you talking about Bart?"

"Whoever. Men aren't always what they seem. Well, I gotta go. I'm working private duty for this strip mall during the holidays and they like me to be seen in every store. The presence of the law keeps down shoplifting."

His words stayed on her mind as he walked away. It was almost as if he knew something more than what he'd said, as if it was Bart that he mistrusted. Not that she blamed him. An old boyfriend shows up out of the blue and stays with a woman eight months pregnant. It must look suspicious to a lot of people. Even she'd had a hard time at first believing his attraction for her was real.

Bart walked over. "You look upset. Is it something your cop friend said?"

"No. I'm just tired and ready to get out of here."

"Good. I understand your need to leave the house, but no more shopping. This place seems safe enough, but I feel a lot better when I control the variables."

"Yes sir." She gave him a little salute and was about to take his arm when her cell phone rang. She slipped it from her pocket and took the call.

"Hello."

"Megan, it's John. Are you all right?"

"Of course. Why do you ask?"

"I got the strangest call a few minutes ago. Some elderly-sounding guy. Said he was your grandfather and that it was urgent that get in touch with you."

"My grandfather's been dead for years. He died right here in Orange Beach."

"That's what I thought. He wanted your phone number but I didn't give it to him."

"Did you get his name and phone number?" she asked, her mind running in frantic circles.

"I would have, but we got disconnected before I had a chance. I figured he'd call back, but he didn't."

"If he does, get the information for me."

"I'll do it."

They'd finished with a short conversation about an up-coming meeting and she broke the connection.

Bart put an arm to her elbow and guided her toward the door. "I take it that it was John again."

"It was. Apparently someone called him trying to get in touch with me. The man said he was my grandfather."

Concern darkened Bart's face. "Let's get out of here. You can fill me in on details in the car."

One of the clerks stopped him as he pushed through the door. "Wait. I have your package."

He thanked her and took the large, bulky bag, but there was no trace of a smile on his face.

Megan finished explaining the message John had given her and then stroked the tight muscles in her neck. "It must have been a crank call, Bart. What else could it have been?"

"I have no idea, and that's what worries me."

"It couldn't have been the man who's been trying to kill me," she reasoned. "He knows where I am."

Bart beat a fist against the steering wheel. "I just wish John had gotten the man's name."

"He will if he calls again." She tried to push the call from her mind as they drove back to the house to spend another afternoon in the cupola, digging for pieces of a puzzle that seemed impossible to solve. It made her dizzy, or else it was merely time for her to eat again.

She reached over and lay a hand on Bart's arm. "Stop at the deli, Bart. I want to run in and pick up some lunch. I'd like to get some cookies to drop off at Fenelda's, too. She seemed so upset after that confrontation with her son."

"Yeah, that Leroy's a real charmer, especially around

his mother. He almost seemed a different guy from the one I met the other day when he came to fix the plumbing.''

''I suspect he was on something this morning. Fenelda admitted to me after he left that he has a drug problem. He was released from a hospital-based addiction program about three months ago.''

''What was he addicted to?''

''She said it ran the gamut—alcohol to crack cocaine. He stayed clean for a while, but she feels certain he's taken up the habit again.''

''He was begging money off your handyman before he left this morning.''

''I guess I've been lucky he didn't steal a few pawnable items from the house the other day when he was working on the plumbing. At least nothing I've noticed. Of course, with all that's going on already, having a few items stolen would be like worrying about a breeze when a hurricane was coming.''

Bart pulled into the deli parking lot, and she crawled out of the car and walked to the door, her protector at her side. Poor Fenelda. The cookies wouldn't be much of a consolation for what she was going through, but doing something nice for her would make Megan feel better.

The baby moved, kicked a few times, and seemed to resettle in a different position as she pushed through the heavy glass door. The baby was kicking less the last few days, probably getting crowded in there. She'd ask the doctor about that when she saw him tomorrow. The baby—due in nine days and still she hadn't called the agency to give them the go-ahead on finding a family to adopt it.

Another woman to take the baby home. Jackie's baby. The baby Megan had nurtured for almost nine months.

The walls of the small bakery begin to close in around her.

"May I help you?"

"No." The word came out as a hoarse whisper. She took a deep breath, determined to pull herself together. "Not yet. I haven't decided."

"Take all the time you need. Let me know when you're ready."

All the time she needed, only the time was running out and her life had fallen into a state of confusion and danger. The only thing she could count on was the wonderful FBI agent who stood just outside the door, always alert, always on duty. And even that couldn't last forever.

"I'll take two dozen of the ladyfingers," she said, making the only decision she seemed capable of making right now.

The Shelby home sat a good fifty yards off the highway, down a dirt road that had more holes than a wool sweater at a moth convention. Bart slowed to a crawl, avoiding the worst of the bumps so as not to send Megan into premature labor. Fenelda's older-model car was parked at the side of the house, behind Leroy's pickup truck. Bart pulled in behind the car.

The house was white clapboard in need of a new coat of paint, but still it had a certain country charm about it. Potted plants stood on either side of the door and a wooden porch swing creaked as it caught a gust of wind.

A flower bed along the front of the house was ablaze with color. Red, pink and purple pansies nodded agreeably as they walked past and a gray cat scooted from its spot by the door. Bart didn't expect any trouble from Leroy here, but he was ready all the same. His gun was out of sight but in easy reach.

He stood back as Megan rang the doorbell. Fenelda

opened the door and smiled tentatively until Megan assured her this was just an impromptu social call.

"We were at the deli and I picked up some cookies for you. I thought you might like them with a cup of coffee." She handed her the white bag.

"You are so thoughtful, just like your grandmother. This is the kind of thing she'd do if she thought I was upset. Will you come in? I'll make some coffee."

Megan nodded. "If you'll make mine water. I'm watching my caffeine intake."

"I never turn down coffee," Bart said, stepping through the door after Megan.

"Excuse the noise," Fenelda apologized as they walked through the living room to the kitchen. "Leroy always has that radio blaring. Day and night. The same music, over and over. But I'd rather he be here than running the streets. I know he's not a kid any longer, but I still worry about him."

"You should make him wear his headphones," Bart suggested. "Save your hearing."

Fenelda took some flowered cups from the cabinet. "It's difficult to make Leroy do anything. He wears them only when he chooses to."

Leroy Shelby. A drug problem. No money. Could he be the man who made attempts on Megan's life? It was possible, though probably too much to ask for. Burt scanned the room as he half listened to Megan and Fenelda chat about Christmases past and how the traditions had changed. Finally, the topic swung back to Leroy. His mother was worried about him, likely with good reason.

Bart tilted his coffee cup, letting the few drops of remaining liquid flow to one side. This was exactly the opportunity he'd been looking for. If he could get with

Leroy when he was under the influence of whatever he'd purchased with Mark's money, he might be able to get something out of him. "I can talk to him. It may not do any good but I've had a little experience with guys trying to break a drug habit."

"I doubt I can even get him to come down the hall to the kitchen," Fenelda said. "He used to respect my wishes, would have done anything I asked him to do, but not anymore."

"Let me try going to his room."

"Help yourself. It's down the hall there." She pointed the way. "Just follow the noise. You can't miss it."

He walked down the hall and knocked at the door. There was no answer. "It's Bart Cromwell, Megan Lancaster's friend. I'd like to talk if you've got a minute." Still no answer. Bart tried the doorknob. It twisted easily in his hand. "Mind if I come in?"

Guess not. He didn't say so. That was all the invitation Bart needed.

The second he opened the door and saw the gun, he knew why Leroy had kept silent.

Chapter Fourteen

Bart stopped in the door and stared at the nauseating sight, his adrenaline kicking in, his suspicions running wild. Leroy was lying across the bed on his back, his legs dangling over the side as if he'd been sitting on the edge and just fell back—fell back into a pool of soggy crimson blood. The head wound gaped open and he knew it was useless to check for signs of life.

A guttural cry and a string of bitter curses tore from his dry throat. No matter how many times he encountered gruesome crime scenes and stared death in the face, he never got used to the feelings that accompanied the sight. Still, he didn't look away until he heard footsteps coming toward him. "Stay back, Megan. You don't want to see this."

"What is it, Bart?"

"Just get back and stay with Fenelda. Keep her away from this room."

Megan ignored his commands. He grabbed her, but not before she peered around him and into the room.

"Oh my God!" She shuddered and gasped for breath before putting her hands over her eyes and collapsing against him. "How do we tell Fenelda?"

"Tell me what?" Fenelda shuffled down the hall, dry-ing her hands on her apron, her sandals slapping against the bare wood.

Bart pulled the door shut and turned to face her. "Come back in the kitchen with me."

Her eyes went wide. "No. It's an overdose, isn't it? Call the ambulance. It's happened before. We have to get him to a hospital, but it will be all right." She was near hysteria and pushing against him, trying to get to her son.

"It's not an overdose, and it's too late to call for an ambulance." It would have been too late even if someone had been there to call the ambulance the second the bullet had sliced through his brain, but that was not a fact he wanted to share just now with the hysterical woman.

"No! Not my boy! I want to see him."

"It's not a good idea, Fenelda." Megan's voice was soft, reassuring. The woman's face went white, but the fight went of her as the words of doom finally singed into her consciousness. Together, one on each side of her heaving body, he and Megan led Fenelda to the kitchen and managed to get her into one of the straight-backed chairs at the table.

This morning he'd hoped Leroy was the man they were looking for, had wanted to put him behind bars and end the dangerous nightmare that threatened Megan's life, but he hadn't wanted to see him dead—not like this. He called the local police from Fenelda's phone and punched in the private number for Luke Powell on his cellular phone. Powell wasn't around to take the call, but Bart left a message as he made his way back to the crime scene before the local police arrived and sent him on his way.

BART MADE a quick assessment. It was either suicide or had been intended to look that way. The gun was on the bed, touching the tips of the fingers of Leroy's right hand.

A printed note was on the table next to the bed, addressed to "Mom." Careful not to contaminate the scene, Bart examined the wound. First appearances indicated that it could well be self-inflicted. A coroner's report would hopefully tell more.

The note was printed in black ink. The pen was still on the table, cap off. He left it lying there while he read.

Mom, I'm sorry to put you through this. It wasn't your fault, so please don't blame yourself. I made bad decisions, but I'm in too deep to get out now. Megan, I'm sorry for the trouble I've caused you and the things I stole. I'm not a killer. It was the drugs that destroyed my decency...

The rest of the note was blurred beyond reading, wet and smeared from the liquid from an overturned glass. He sniffed and picked up the odor of whiskey. He looked around the room. No evidence of a struggle. Nothing out of place. Only an overturned glass of whiskey and a dead body on the bed, a Smith & Wesson .38 touching the limp fingers as if it had just fallen from their grasp.

Bart pulled a small notebook from his pocket and copied Leroy's note, then jotted down a few details to help him remember the room exactly as he'd found it. An obvious suicide, and Bart never trusted the obvious.

A squeal of approaching sirens cut into his thoughts. The investigation would all be cut-and-dried. The confession was right there—in black and white for anyone to see.

"Son of a bitch! It's Leroy Shelby, all right."

Bart backed away from the bed as two uniformed policemen stepped in the door.

"Shot his own brains out," the younger cop said. "We

should bring the high school out here on a field trip. One look at this would make them think twice about using drugs.'' He liberally sprinkled a few four-letter words into his comments.

The older cop's gaze left the body and focused on Bart. ''Are you the guy who found the body?''

''I'm afraid so.''

''That ought to give you some good nightmare material.''

''Yeah, I guess it will.'' Only he wasn't worried about the image disturbing his sleep. He had a lot worse roaming around the hidden crevices of his gray matter. It was Fenelda Shelby he hurt for. And Megan, at a time she should be concentrating on nothing but giving birth to a healthy baby.

''Stick around,'' the gray-haired cop said. ''I'll need to talk to you, though it looks like a 10-56.''

''Looks can sometimes be deceiving,'' Bart offered, sure the cops wouldn't be interested in the input of a car salesman.

''If it's not a suicide, we'll know it. Are you a friend of the victim's?''

''No, but I've met him a time or two at Megan Lancaster's house.''

''So you're Megan's friend, the one Roger Collier mentioned.'' The man nodded and smiled as if he were in on a juicy secret.

''I'm a friend of Megan's.''

''Just hang around a minute so I can take your statement. After that, you'll be free to go.''

The younger cop had already found and picked up the note. ''Definitely a suicide,'' he announced. ''Tough go to do it right in your own bed, but then I guess he won't be sleeping in here tonight and he won't be the one cleaning up the mess.''

"We'll need to get some pictures, just in case there are questions later. Get the position of the body and the gun, and dust the gun and that glass that's turned over for prints.''

Bart left them to their work and walked back to the kitchen, wishing he was the one conducting the investigation, wishing there were no rules, no formalities, no string of command. But he was undercover and had been given no authorization to identify himself, much less to offer services that probably weren't wanted.

Fenelda was sobbing softly when he stepped into the kitchen and Megan was on the phone explaining to someone what had happened. He walked to the coffeepot and poured a cup, then went back and sat down at the table.

Fenelda blew her nose and sniffled. "I tried to bring him up right. I took him to Sunday school all his life.''

Bart lay a hand on top of hers, for the first time noticing the extended veins and thin, corded lines that ran from her wrists to her fingertips. They were hardworking hands. Reminded him of his mom's, and he had the sudden urge to give her a call and tell her he loved her.

"I'm sure he knew you loved him, Mrs. Shelby. It's just that once a guy gets on those drugs, they can fall into a downward spiral that they can't pull out of.''

"His dad was a good man. He did all he could to take care of us. This would've broken his heart.''

The way it was breaking hers. "Remember the good times, Mrs. Shelby. My mom always says that the best way to make it through the hard times is to remember the happy ones.''

She sniffled again and wiped her eyes with the corner

of her apron. "I'll miss him so much. For all the bad he did, he's still my son."

Bart was thankful when Megan joined them at the table. He'd never been good at this.

"I talked to Reverend Forrester. He's on his way over and he'll let the women of the church know what's happened."

"Thank you, Megan. You're like your grandmother, so sweet. Always taking time to think of everyone else. Your mother was a constant vexation to her, wanting and never giving, but you were the light of her life."

Bart's cell phone rang. He excused himself and walked out the door and into the backyard to take the call. As he expected, it was from Luke. He filled him in on the latest news.

"This would explain the attempts on Megan's life," Luke said when he'd finished reading him the copy of the note. "A drug addict trying to hide his crimes and keep from going to jail. I hadn't had a chance to tell you yet, but his background check turned up two prior convictions. The judge wasn't likely to let him off with a hospital stay after the third arrest."

"I know it makes sense."

"But you don't buy it."

"I didn't say that."

"You didn't have to."

"So this is why I never win at poker with you guys." He bent to pat a tail-wagging black dog who'd just come running up, likely one who'd just lost his master. "It's the timing that worries me. Joshua Caraway breaks out of jail. Ben Brewster's house is bombed and he and his wife are killed. A month later, there are attacks on the woman who is carrying Jackie and Ben's child. Two events I might buy coincidence. Three...you gotta admit there's cause for suspicion.''

''Only we don't know that Ben's house was bombed. And Megan's problems didn't start until she came back to Pelican's Roost, where someone had been stealing from her beach house to support an escalating habit. And don't forget that Ben's mom, the obvious one to go after next, if you've vowed to kill a man and his family, has had no trouble at all.''

''You're right. I'm just hardheaded, slow to let go of a theory once it gets hold of me.''

''Or perhaps it's Megan Lancaster you don't want to let go of.''

As far as Bart was concerned, that was a given. He didn't want her out of his life, but he wasn't sure he was going to have a say in the matter. She liked him a lot, maybe even loved him. But she was so afraid of commitment that she was about to give away a baby she definitely loved. That didn't bode well for him. Only she couldn't just give him up without any explanation. If she didn't want him in her life, she'd have to tell him so up front. Only then would he move on.

In fact, he wasn't going to let her give up either of them without an explanation—for herself as well as for him.

MEGAN WALKED through the old beach house, opening cupboards and drawers and realizing for the first time how little she knew of what she actually owned. Her grandmother had delineated in her will which pieces of her more valuable jewelry were to go to Megan's mother and which were to go to Megan, but other valuables simply remained with the house.

Silver, crystal, a coin collection, a few original paintings. She'd never had most of them appraised, and the only indication of their worth she had was the list included in her grandmother's will. Several items were gone including her gold bangle bracelet and a necklace she hadn't missed until now.

"What's the damage?" Bart asked, joining her in the room that had been her grandmother's bedroom.

"It looks to be no more than five thousand dollars to me, certainly not enough to kill for. The truth is, I would probably have lent him this much if he'd asked."

"To buy drugs?"

"No, I guess not. It's such a waste of a life. Poor Fenelda. She's going to have a hard time coping with this. Luckily she has some good friends who'll stand by her and give what comfort they can."

"I'm just glad you weren't killed in his plunge to the depths. It's bad enough you had to go through the trauma of his foiled attempts on your life."

"And now it's over. Life can go on, and I must say I'm glad this is not connected to Jackie. Her death was bad enough, but I couldn't bear to think that she'd been murdered."

Bart looked over her shoulder at the list of missing items. "I'd like to have a look at that list when you're through, with as many identifying details about each item as you can supply. I'll check the local pawnshops and see what I can locate. He probably didn't go too far to dump it."

"It would be nice to get these items back, not so much for me. I hadn't even missed anything except my bracelet, but for my grandmother."

"I'll see what I can do."

"I know. You always do. I couldn't have made it through all this without you. And you wouldn't have been here at all if it hadn't been for Joshua Caraway's escaping jail. Brutal, paid assassin or not, he was responsible for bringing you into my life.''

She turned and stepped into his arms. He had come into her life, made her feel more attractive and alive than any man had ever made her feel before. Only now it was over. Tonight, tomorrow, two days down the stretch, he'd be packing his little black suitcase they'd picked up in his condo a couple of weeks ago and he'd drive away.

The baby moved inside her, as if it was curling up into a tiny ball and then stretching its arms and legs, taking up every centimeter of space in her crowded womb.

The baby and Bart. The sense of loss was overwhelming, consuming, suffocating. She clasped her stomach as a sharp pain attacked the small of her back.

Bart held her at arm's length. ''Is something wrong? Is it the baby?''

She struggled for a deep breath. ''My first contraction. False labor, I imagine, but I think I better sit down, and I could use a glass of water.''

He helped her to the four-poster bed a few feet away. ''Stay right here until I get back.'' He bent and slipped the loafers from her feet, then propped her feet on the bed as if she were an invalid.

She lay perfectly still, hardly daring to breathe. She was not ready for the baby to come. She still had to make the all-important call to the adoption agency. She stared at the phone by the bed, reached out and picked up the receiver. She knew the number by heart, but her fingers refused to follow her brain's commands.

Instead, they followed her heart's. She cradled her oversize belly in her hands. ''Oh, sweetie. Don't make this so hard on me. I can't be your mommy. I can't. It wouldn't be fair to you.''

BART STOPPED at the door to the family room where Megan was stretched out on the sofa. It was less that an hour past sunset, but the air had a December chill to it, and he'd already built a blazing fire in the fireplace. The only lights in the room were the twinkling bulbs on the decorated tree, and they mingled with the fire's glow to paint the room in mystical golden hues.

A beautiful pregnant woman, who was intelligent, sensitive, caring and extremely sensual, living right here in paradise. And tonight he'd probably lose it all. Whoever said it was better to have loved and lost than not to have loved at all was obviously a masochist.

"Who was on the phone?" Megan asked as he stepped into the room."

"Luke Powell."

"Good news this time, I hope."

"He has evidence that Joshua Caraway headed straight for St. Louis when he escaped and stayed there until he went to Chicago where his friends were making arrangements to fly him out of the country. If they hadn't caught him when they did, he'd be in South America by now."

"Then there's no reason not to believe that Leroy Shelby was behind the attempts on my life."

"Apparently not."

She exhaled sharply. "Then the nightmare is finally over." She moved her gaze from his face to the wrapped package he held in his hands. "What's that?"

"An early Christmas present."

"So that was what was in the package the clerk handed you at the store this afternoon. You are sneaky, but you can't give presents early, Bart Cromwell."

"Sure I can. Close your eyes and get ready."

First a kiss. Then a present that was going to force a couple of issues he was certain she was not ready to face.

But time was running out. The baby was due in less than a week. And his legitimate reasons for being in Orange Beach had already expired.

He took her in his arms and touched his lips to hers. His need for her rocked through him with the force of a Gulf storm.

Chapter Fifteen

Megan felt Bart's lips on hers, and as always the thrill started there and worked its way to the top of her head and the tips of her toes. Eyes closed tightly, she reached up and wrapped her hands around his neck, deepening the kiss. "My kind of surprise," she whispered.

"Then open your eyes and see the real present."

She followed his instructions, sorry the second she did. He was holding a baby's toy, a cuddly brown teddy bear with dark beaded eyes that seemed to be condemning her. Her chest tightened painfully and she looked away. Slowly, the way she did everything these days, she moved her feet to the floor and pulled to a sitting position. "You shouldn't have."

"Every baby needs a teddy bear."

"And I'm sure the baby's parents, whoever they turn out to be, will buy her one." He tried to hand it to her, but she pulled away.

He dropped to the sofa beside her and splayed the fingers of his right hand across her stomach, slowly stoking the stretched skin through the light fabric of her smock. It was impossible to stay upset with him, and yet she had to let him know he'd overstepped his bounds.

She sighed and lay her hands on top of his. "Why are you doing this, Bart?"

"I wanted to buy the baby her first toy. Is that so terrible?"

"I can't keep the baby. I told you that. I'd make a lousy mother."

"I know that's what you say."

"It's not what I *say*. It's the way it is." Her voice was shaking. She was shaking. "My job takes all my time."

"With your skills, you can have a million jobs."

"What's that supposed to mean?"

"Just that this isn't about your job. It's about you and your misguided perception of yourself. You're afraid you don't have enough love, but you overflow with it."

"You waltzed into my life days ago. You can't begin to make that kind of judgment about me."

"I know you gave your body to carry a friend's baby. That's the most loving and unselfish act I know. It's not something a man would do, even if we could. I know you loved Jackie and your grandmother, and even your mother, though she wasn't able to give you the kind of security and affection you craved."

Her insides quaked and she felt as if the blood was rushing from her head, leaving her dizzy and weak. "But you're talking about a baby, a tiny, defenseless human being. I don't have what it takes to give her all the love and care she needs."

"You'd make a fabulous mother. If you don't want this baby, that's one thing, Megan. But don't give her up out of fear, out of some sense that you don't deserve her and can't give her the stability your mother failed to give you."

She got up from the couch and walked to the window. The waves were crashing into the sand, the fierceness matching the tangled fervor of her emotions. "This isn't your concern, Bart."

"Fine, Megan. If you don't want the baby, give her up. There are plenty of families who'll want her." He picked up the phone and brought it to her. "Call the adoption agency and tell them you have a baby for them. Ask them to find parents who'll learn to love Jackie's child the way you already do."

She yanked the phone from his hand and punched in the three-number exchange of the number she knew by heart. Her fingers grew numb, refused to function. Tears burned the back of her eyelids and her hands started to shake.

Bart took the phone from her hands and hurled it to the nearest chair as he took her in his arms. "Oh, Megan. I don't want to hurt you, but I can't just stand by and watch you give up the future because of a past you can't change."

"This has nothing to do with my past."

"Okay." He cradled her against him, stroking her back, kissing the top of her head.

"I can't change who I am, Bart. If I try, it will be a disaster. I can't do that to an innocent baby."

"What about to me, Megan. When this is over, will you toss me from your life the same way?"

"Don't be ridiculous."

"It doesn't seem ridiculous to me. You're afraid of commitment, so I can't imagine that you're going to fit me into your life, that you'll work to have a future with me."

A future? She couldn't think about that now. Couldn't deal with anything beyond having the baby. "Please, Bart. I can't think or talk about commitment. My life is in flux. I can't deal with forever now."

"And I can't settle for less." He let go of her and backed away. "I'll stay until after the baby's born, Megan, unless you'd rather I leave. I'm not as good at this love-for-the-moment stuff as you are."

"I want you with me, Bart."

"For now." He pushed a lock of hair from her face and tucked it behind her ear. "Just make sure we get to a hospital on time. I don't deliver babies."

"I'll bet you could, Bart Cromwell, or whoever you are. I'll bet you could do anything you set your mind to."

"No. I can't build a life with a woman who's afraid to love." He turned and walked from the room, and the walls seemed to close in around her. What she really wanted was to hold him close and tell him that she loved him.

Instead, she watched him walk away.

December 20

THE DRIVE HOME from the doctor's office was quiet. What should have been a day of celebrating had dissolved into an awkward silence, the first Megan and Bart had experienced together since the day he'd moved into Pelican's Roost.

The baby was fine, due one week to the day. Megan had still not made the call to the adoption agency, but she planned to follow through with the task when they got back to the house. No matter how hard it was to make the call, it had to be done.

Bart had spent the morning on the phone, calling pawnshops in the area. He'd located Megan's bracelet and a silver coffee service that had belonged to her grandmother in a shop in Foley, Alabama. He'd gone immediately to pick them up. He'd shown the man a photograph of Leroy

Shelby and the clerk had identified him as the man who had hocked the items.

After weeks of mystery and danger, closure was taking shape. Now there was nothing left but a slow, swelling sense of loss growing deep inside Megan's soul. She was giving up the baby, and she felt as if she was losing Bart as well. The emotions were familiar—the same ones she'd experienced all her life, every time she and her mother had packed their belongings in a worn suitcase and moved to a new town.

Only this time it went much deeper, burned inside her like a relentless fire that wouldn't let up. Even thinking of her job did nothing to ease the pain. She turned to Bart, as always amazed by the feelings that surged inside her when she glimpsed the rugged lines of his profile.

"I guess the FBI case is officially closed," she said.

"It will be as soon as I write up the final report."

"And Bart Cromwell will dissolve into a name on a file."

"Afraid so. You missed your chance at getting a good deal on a car."

"I didn't feel like driving to Nashville anyway. So tell me about the real you. Is he as fascinating as the man I've been living with?"

"Depends on what you call exciting. My name's Dirk Cason. I'm an Iowa farm boy, oldest of six kids, red-necked, and I can peel an ear of corn before you can whistle the opening chords of 'Dixie.'"

He smiled and tipped his faded baseball cap, and she went weak. "I want to hear all about you and your family."

"Are you sure? That could take a while."

"I'm sure. Start with your siblings. I can't imagine growing up with a houseful of brothers and sisters."

"It wasn't all fun and games, but we had some great times. Still do. Buck's the youngest. He's still in college, but he wants to go into the FBI when he graduates. Sarah's next, happily married with three children, all girls. And then there's Maria, the sister I built the dollhouse for. She's in med school.

"Last, but not least, there's the twins, Jude and Jacob, two years younger than me."

Megan settled back in the car seat and listened to his stories of childhood pranks and holidays, of nieces and nephews and fishing trips. A world as foreign to her as one from a science-fiction novel. A world she was certain she'd never fit into.

Sandra Birney was waiting for them when they returned to Pelican's Roost. Her car was parked in back of the house and she was perched in the rocker on the front balcony, waving at them as Bart pulled in behind her car.

"Wonder what she wants," Bart asked. "It must be important if she waited around for you."

"It can't be bad news. Surely we've drained that well dry by now."

MEGAN SPOTTED the blinking light on the answering machine when they walked through the door. "I have a message," she said, staring at the phone. "I better check it. It could be important."

"It's probably Fenelda," Sandra said, stepping through the door in front of Bart. "She's having a hard time with all of this. She's certain she let Leroy down. The truth is, I've never seen a woman try harder to keep a boy on the straight and narrow. He just fell into a ditch and couldn't find his way out."

"But it can't be easy losing a son." Megan punched the button and waited for the message. It was John's voice that blared into the room. "I had another call from the old gentleman claiming to be your grandfather, but this time I got his name and phone number. The name is Carlisle Sellers and he's in a hospital in Birmingham, Alabama. He says it's urgent that he talk to you."

Megan scribbled down the number as John gave it, confusion playing games in her mind. When the message finished, she turned to Bart. "I have no idea who this man is that keeps calling my office, but it's not my grandfather."

Sandra exhaled sharply. "Carlisle Sellers is Lane Sellers's father, Jackie's grandfather."

"It can't be," Megan insisted. "Her grandfather died a few months after her dad died. I remember how upset Jackie was to lose two people she loved so close together. She was studying abroad that semester, trying to escape the grief of her father's death, and couldn't even get back for the funeral."

Sandra went the Christmas tree and absently straightened a glass ball on one of its branches. "All I know is that Carlisle is Lane's dad."

Bart walked over and stood in front of her, the muscles in his face and neck tense. "If you know something about this, Sandra, you owe it to Megan to tell her. She's been through enough the past month."

She shook her head. "I can't say more."

"But you know more." Bart insisted.

"You have the man's number. Call him."

Still, it didn't make sense. "Why would Jackie's mother tell her that her grandfather had died if he was still alive? I know she didn't like the man, but she couldn't have been that cruel."

Sandra put her hand on Megan's arm. "Janelle had her reasons, Megan. Everyone has reasons for what they do.

No matter what you learn from Carlisle Sellers, just remember that. Now, I have to go.''

"You just got here.'' Megan took off her light jacket and tossed it on the sofa. "You can't leave without even saying why you came by.''

"No reason. I was just in the neighborhood and wanted to check in on you. I know what a shock it must have been being at Fenelda's yesterday when Bart found the body. I'll call you later.'' She opened the door, then stopped. "Remember what I said, Megan, about people having their reasons. And no matter what you think when this is over, your mother loves you.''

"How did my mother get into this discussion?''

Sandra didn't answer. Instead, she gave a little wave and left them standing and watching her hurry depart. "Do you have any idea what that's all about?'' Megan asked, once Sandra had started down the steps that led to the beach.

"I guess there's only one way to find out.'' Bart picked up the number she'd scribbled on the pad next to the phone. "Do you want me to get Carlisle Sellers on the line for you?''

"Why not?''

She dropped to the sofa as Bart punched in the number for the hospital in Birmingham, the newest information jumping into melee in her mind. If Jackie's grandfather was still alive, why was he trying to reach her? And why had Sandra brought her mother into this, cautioned Megan not to judge her too harshly?

She waited and watched the changing expression on Bart's face as he talked. A few seconds later, he broke the connection and slid next to her on the couch.

"Apparently, Carlisle Sellers has taken a turn for the worse. The nurse said he's fallen into a semi-coma.''

"What's wrong with him?"

"Heart problems. He's eighty-six. She said he fades in and out of consciousness, but when he's awake he's lucid." He took her hand in his. "He's on the critical list, not expected to make it through the week."

"Poor man. He was probably confused when he said he was my grandfather. I'm sure it was Jackie he was looking for. I'd love to go and visit him, but I'm in no shape to drive to Birmingham before the baby comes, and after I deliver, it will likely be too late."

"If you want, I can drive up and try to talk to him."

"Oh, Bart. Please do. It's the only way I'll be able to find out if this is really Jackie's grandfather."

"I'll leave first thing in the morning. That way I should get back by sunset. I don't want to leave you alone at night."

"It may be a wasted trip. There's no guarantee he'll come out of the coma."

"I'll chance it."

Megan stared out the glass door, seeking comfort from the endless movement of the water. "If it is him, think how sad it will be if he and Jackie lost all those years when they could have gotten to know one another better. Years when she believed he was dead."

He put an arm around her shoulder and held her close. "You're right. People should never let anything keep them from being with someone they love."

The words seared into her heart, slicing the way a jagged knife would tear into flesh. She was about to give up a baby that she already dearly loved. And she was about to return to a life that didn't include Bart. Only, for her, there was really no other way.

"I'm glad you're going to wait until morning, Bart."

"If you're afraid to stay alone, I'm sure we can find someone to stay with you."

"I'm not afraid. I just want another night in your arms." Another night and all the memories she could store.

His lips touched hers and she melted against him. She pushed all thoughts of Leroy and Jackie and Carlisle Sellers from her mind. She didn't want to think at all. She only wanted to feel.

THE YOUNG MAN SAT on the beach, a cigarette between his lips, the smoke blowing away on the Gulf breeze. The plan had worked to perfection. The cops had bought it like the dopes they were.

Suicide.

Only he'd been the one who'd written the note and pulled the trigger. He'd had no choice. Leroy knew too much and he couldn't be trusted. One slip of his drugged tongue and it would have all been over.

Instead of sitting on the beach tonight contemplating his glowing future, he'd be in jail, waiting for a trial and a one-way ticket to death row for the murders of Ben and Jackie Brewster and the attempted murder of Megan Lancaster. Only now the murder would not be a foiled attempt but the real thing. The Sellerses would all be dead. All but him.

"Sorry, Megan, but your mother was a bitch, and now you're going to pay the price. An unfortunate accident to an awkward, cumbersome pregnant woman. No one will suspect a thing."

Plop. One dead body smashed into the sand.

The image amused him. He couldn't wait to bring it to life. And he would, no matter who else he had to kill in the process. Time was running out. The old man would die soon.

Chapter Sixteen

December 21

Bart kept a heavy foot on the accelerator as he headed the car back to Orange Beach and Pelican's Roost. He'd just talked to Megan and she was doing fine. No contractions. Still he was anxious to get back.

The trip to the hospital had taken longer than he'd expected, mainly because he'd sat in the hospital room until Carlisle Sellers had finally come to enough to talk to him. And talk he had, spilling out secrets that had stayed hidden for years.

A story the old gentleman didn't want on his conscience as he prepared to meet his maker. Secrets that would have no doubt set Orange Beach on it's heels if they had come out thirty years ago. Even now, Bart wasn't sure how Megan was going to take the news that the person she'd always thought of as her best friend was really her half sister.

Bart would have to be the one to tell her. And the good news was that the doctor believed that Carlisle Sellers would stay alive long enough to see the great-grandchild that came from one granddaughter's egg and grew in another granddaughter's body.

If all of this had come out earlier, he'd have been sure that the fact that Megan was about to inherit a large sum of money was behind the attempts on her life. Megan and Jackie and a nephew, the son of Carlisle's ne'er-do-well son. All part of the family.

A nephew who stood to get a lot more cash with Jackie and Megan out of the picture. A motive to kill the both of them. The thoughts rumbled inside him. Leroy Shelby had confessed to the attempts on Megan's life and taken his own life.

Or had he?

Suicides could be faked, and there had not even been a handwriting analysis of the note. Simply a visual scan. Doubt and suspicions grappled with the facts as he knew them, spurred on by a burst of adrenaline and years of dealing with depraved acts and nefarious minds.

Anxiety pitched in his stomach and he wished like hell that the other agents in Orange Beach hadn't left town this morning. He couldn't change that, so he grabbed the cellular phone and punched in the number for information. A second later he had Roger Collier on the other end.

"Hi, Roger. This is Bart Cromwell, Megan's friend."

"Yeah. I remember you."

"I had to drive up to Birmingham today and I'm running a little later than I expected. I just talked to Megan and she's fine, but I hate for her to be by herself. Would you mind going over there and staying with her until I get back to town? I should be more than an hour. I'll be glad to pay you for your services."

"You mean stay with her in a police capacity?"

"That's right."

"Are you expecting some kind of trouble? I thought it was all over with Leroy's death."

He had to handle this carefully. He didn't want Roger going over and frightening Megan needlessly, but he wanted him prepared for anything. "I'm just concerned that Leroy might have had a partner and that the guy might go back to see what else he could steal. I don't want a thief breaking into the house with Megan there."

"I wouldn't worry about that. We didn't find anything to indicate that Leroy had an accomplice."

"All the same, I'd appreciate you staying with her. But don't frighten her, just tell her I was worried and asked you to drop over and stay with her."

"Will do, but I think it's a waste of time, and you don't have to pay me. Megan's a friend."

"How quickly can you get there?"

"Ten minutes at the most."

"Good."

Bart kept his foot to the pedal. Even with Roger on the job, he was anxious to get back to the beach, back to Megan. He'd had time to do some serious thinking while he sat in the hospital room watching Mr. Sellers fight for every breath.

He'd made up his mind then that he was not giving up on Megan, not until the day he became convinced that she would never love him the way he loved her. A few things in life were worth fighting for. Megan Lancaster was at the top of his list.

MEGAN HUNG UP the phone. She'd finally made the call to the adoption agency that she should have made weeks ago. It didn't hurt the way she'd expected it to. Mostly she felt numb, drained of emotion. And alone, even though Roger Collier was downstairs reading some book on true crime that he'd brought with him.

His presence was totally unnecessary, but she appreciated Bart's concern. For a tough FBI agent, he was easily the most thoughtful and considerate man she'd ever been around.

One day without him, and she missed him desperately. Missed his heavy footsteps, missed his singing along with the CD in his deep male voice. Missed the smell of him, all musk and spice and soap. Missed his touch when they passed in the hall, and the taste of him when they kissed.

But missing him was soon to be a fact of life. The baby was due on December twenty-seventh. After that, she'd rest for a week or so, then go back to work. Fly to London, get caught up in meetings and negotiations and making decisions that affected the company's bottom line. Bart would take on his next assignment, become a different man in a different town with different crimes to claim his mind. He'd never really been Bart Cromwell at all, though he still was Bart in her mind.

He believed she couldn't commit to a relationship because of her past, and maybe he was right. But even if they promised to stay close, it wouldn't work. Their lives were too different. They'd drift apart and she'd be left on her own again.

Not knowing why, except that she felt drawn to the past this afternoon, she began to climb the stairs at the end of the hall. She called down to Roger. "I'm going to the cupola. Tell Bart where I am if he gets back before I come downstairs."

"Do you want me to go with you?"

"No. I'll be fine."

"If you need me, just give a yell. I'll be right here."

The sun was already starting its final plunge as she

opened the door and stepped inside the round room, painting the undersides of scattered clouds in glorious streaks of orange. A few people were out walking, enjoying the sunset, but they'd retreat into the warmth of their houses and condos by dark.

Still breathing heavy from the exertion of the climb, she stood and stared at the boxes. She couldn't lift the ones from the top of the stack, but Bart had left a few of them on the floor, thinking they'd be back to rummage through them. She chose the one labeled "Marilyn." The tape was old and tore easily with just the pressure of her fingernails.

The box was full of clothes. She pulled out the garments one by one. Skirts and sweaters from the sixties, the kind of items that sold for big bucks now in vintage-clothing shops. She ran her fingers along the crinkly edge of a blue taffeta formal with a tiny waist and a neckline that dipped seductively low.

She imagined her grandmother's disapproval, could all but see her shaking her head and frowning as Megan's mother twirled in the full-skirted dress, showing off her shapely body.

Megan reached deeper into the box, and this time her fingers rustled the pages of a book. She pulled it out and stared at it. The cover was a faded green burlap, ragged on the edges. A brass lock was still clasped shut, but the fabric holding the lock had ripped lose.

A diary. Just holding it in her hands made her feel as if she was snooping into her mother's private life. The book held words and thoughts from the past, a glimpse into the heart and mind of a woman who still seemed like a stranger to Megan. Perhaps reading a few pages would give her some much-needed insight. Hands trembling, she opened the cover and read the first line, written in perfect penmanship.

I entered the Miss Shrimp Festival Pageant today. I haven't told Mother yet. She'll have a fit when I do, say it's not proper for a young lady to prance around and show off her body. I plan not only to prance, but to win. This pageant, and lots more. I want to go all the way to the top, stand on the stage and have them crown me Miss America. That will be my ticket to Broadway.

Megan flipped the pages, skimming through the book until the word *pregnant* jumped out at her. The penmanship was not as perfect on this page. The writing was shaky and the ink in some spots had been blurred as if someone had spilled something on it, or shed a few tears.

I'm two weeks late for my period. I haven't told anyone but Sandra, but I know I'm pregnant. Mother will kill me when I tell her, especially if she finds out who the father is. She'll never understand that I love him and he loves me. It's only his wicked wife who comes between us.

But it's Daddy I hate to tell most of all. It will break his heart and I'll never be his precious little girl again.

For the first time in her life, Megan had some sense of what it must have been like for her mother. Young. Afraid. Pregnant by a married man.

Which meant that everything her mother had ever told her about her father had been a lie, except perhaps the part that he'd wanted no part of Megan's mother or her.

She read on as if in a trance, as the young girl behind the story seemed to step from the musty covers of the diary.

Tears fell from Megan's eyes and ran down her cheeks as she read the entries that covered the following weeks and months. Her mother had been devastated by the rejection of the man she loved. She'd dealt with her father's pain at his little girl's condition and her mother's reproach. She'd grown up fast, from spoiled, little girl to single parent.

But as heartbroken as Megan's mother had been, she'd kept the man's identity a secret from her grandmother, not even writing his name in the diary. But afraid, ashamed, her spirit broken, she'd still wanted to keep her baby. She'd wanted Megan, though she'd been emotionally and financially unprepared for the challenge of becoming a single parent.

Megan closed the diary, feeling a stronger kinship with her mother than she'd ever felt before. Her mother was who she was, a composite of all the things that had happened to her and a personality formed by a father who doted on her and a community that valued beauty far too highly.

That was Megan's mother, but it wasn't her. She circled her stomach with her hands as sweet relief rushed her senses. "I was wrong, little one. I'm far stronger than my mother has ever been. I won't give you away—not ever. I love you so much and I'll be a good mother. I will. And even when I make mistakes, I'll get over it and so will you."

John would think she was crazy to give up her career, but it didn't matter what John thought. It only mattered that Megan reached out and grabbed life. She wanted this baby and she wanted a chance at happy-ever-after with Bart. She wanted it all, and she was going after it.

Heavy footsteps sounded on the stairs leading to the cupola. It must be Bart. She stood and walked to the door, her heart singing. Now that she'd made up her mind to go for the gusto, she couldn't wait to throw her arms around him and warn him that he was in for a lifetime of loving the likes of which he'd never known before.

She opened the door, but it was Mark Cox who climbed toward her. "What are you doing here?" she asked.

"Finishing what I started in Atlanta a month ago."

Chapter Seventeen

"Don't look so surprised, Megan. It's a small world. You never know who'll show up with a few carpentry tools. Or a bomb."

Mark's words seared into Megan's mind as panic thundered through her senses. "What are you talking about?"

"You know what I'm talking about. I can see the fright shining in your eyes." He wrapped his strong hands around her arms, his fingers digging into her flesh. "You know what's coming, don't you?"

"Why are you doing this?"

"Because I'm Mark Sellers Cox, the legitimate heir to our grandfather's money. You, my pretty, pregnant slut, are the trash that came into the family through the back door. That's why I have to kill you."

His words made no sense, but the one fact she grasped was that he was here to kill her and the baby. He was at least six feet of brute strength. She was big and cumbersome, slow on her feet. Her gaze scanned the circular room, looking for anything to help even out the odds. There was nothing.

She'd have to use her brain. Have to think of a way to stop him.

"I deserve the Sellers family fortune, and it's time I finally get what I deserve."

Money. That was it. He thought she was trying to get money for the baby. "You can have all the Sellerses' money, if there is any," she pleaded. "I won't claim a cent for the baby."

"The baby? I'm not worried about the kid. It's you who I have no intention of splitting the money with. You've already gotten your share anyway."

"I don't know what you're talking about."

"I'm talking about your sleazebag of a mother who slept around with a married man and then took money from the stupid son of a bitch's father just to keep the story quiet."

"Do you know who my father is?"

"Oh, yeah. I always knew. It was the big family secret. Janelle Sellers would have killed me. So I kept quiet, protected you and your mother and Lane Sellers."

"Lane Sellers?"

"Yeah. Don't tell me you didn't know."

Jackie's father. No wonder her grandmother hadn't wanted them to be friends. No wonder Janelle Sellers had hated that her daughter chose Megan as her confidante.

"You and Jackie got it all. I was the son of the black sheep and I got nothing. But I'll make up for it now. I'll be the sole survivor of the Sellers clan."

"But your last name is Cox. Bart looked you up. You have a record for DWI's and possession of drugs."

"Cox is my stepfather's name. The only thing he ever gave me."

Slowly the pieces of the puzzle slid into the distorted image. "You're the one who planted a bomb and blew Jackie and Ben to kingdom come. You did it for money."

"Who me? The explosion was an accident. Don't you read the newspapers?"

Anger, hate, fury, contempt. She felt it all and it turned her inside out, made her sick at her stomach and made it impossible to even look at the man digging his clammy fingers into her arm.

"Don't worry, Megan. I have no intention of blowing you up. We're just going to take a stroll out on the widow's walk. Too bad that you're so misshapen, so clumsy. You'll fall right over the top of the railing. Fall. And fall. And fall. Until your big pregnant body splatters on the sand."

He pushed her toward the door. She tried to break away, but he yanked her arm behind her back, twisting until the pain wracked her body and tears stung her eyes. He opened the door with his other hand and shoved her onto the narrow walkway.

The wind slapped her in the face, and she gasped for breath as he forced her toward the balustrade. "Look down, Megan. See how far it is. But you'll fall quickly. It will be so sad. The same way it was sad when Leroy put a bullet through his brain."

"You killed him, too, didn't you? You killed him to cover up the failed attempts on my life."

"That and to get that undercover cop out of the way. A nice story the two of you came up with. Most people even bought it. I did for a while, until I put two and two together, finally realized why you never left the house without him. I should have known that no man would fall for a woman with a stomach like a beach ball."

No man would fall for a pregnant woman. Only Bart had. He'd seen beyond her body, had found something in her to love. Now she had to find a way to stay alive. For him and the baby. And for a chance at the kind of happiness she'd never dreamed she'd find.

"Now even the cop left you."

"Roger Collier is downstairs. He'll know you were up here. You'll never get away with this."

He laughed, a raucous, taunting laugh that hinted of madness. "Roger Collier won't be talking. Not today. Not ever again."

He'd killed him, and if he'd killed an armed policeman, what chance did she have against him?

"When they find Roger dead, they'll connect it to you."

"You're wrong, Megan. Dead wrong. They'll never find the body. I'll take it with me when I go."

"You're not kin to Jackie. You'll never get the Sellerses' money." She was stalling for time now, throwing out any accusation to keep him talking until Bart arrived.

"Oh, I'm kin all right. The nephew, from the poor white trash side of the family. My dad was the black sheep who left home one day and never came back. My mother eventually moved away and had nothing to do with my grandfather or Jackie's parents. She never liked Lane or Janelle anyway. But I wised up, made lots of trips to see my grandfather over the past few years, which is more than Jackie did. He's assured me I'm in the will. When he dies, I'll just show up and get the check."

"How did you know where to find me?"

"I started coming back here years ago, long before I knew it would come down to this. I did work for the people around town without ever letting on that I had lived here as a child. And everyone knows the Lancasters own Pelican's Roost. The rambling old beach house with the charming cupola and the widow's walk."

Megan looked down and grew dizzy. One little push

was all it would take to make her lose her balance and go flying over the railing. The wind howled, drowning out every sound except the rapid pounding of her heart.

Mark's grasp tightened and she knew it was almost over. Over for her and for the baby. Bart would find her body and think she fell. No one would ever know the truth, and Mark Cox would get away with multiple murders.

The happiness she'd come so close to grabbing was slipping from her grasp. Mark's body pressed against hers, and she felt his hands slide from her arms to her breasts. "One little push, Megan, and it will all be over."

BART STAMPED HIS FEET at the door, knocking the sand loose from his shoes. It was almost dark, but the good thing was, Megan wasn't here alone. The carpenter's truck was in the driveway and so was Roger Collier's squad car.

"I'm back," he called as he fit his key into the door and pushed it open. He waited for an answer, but the house was quiet. Megan was probably resting in her bedroom, but where was Roger Collier?

The answer hit him square in the face as he stepped into the kitchen. Roger's head was on the table, his arms dangling lifelessly from his drooped body. Two ends of a frayed rope fell from his neck like a knotted tie.

Heart pounding, he drew his gun and bounded up the stairs. "Megan. Megan!" His own voice echoed in his head as fear split him in half. The carpenter. Mark Cox. Was he dead, too, or was he the other Sellers heir? Here under their noses all the time?

He walked from room to room, searching, half expecting Mark to jump from behind every closed door. But all he found were empty rooms and increasing horror. He couldn't be too late. God, don't let him be too late.

A rush of cold air brushed his face as he stepped past the stairwell to the cupola and felt a rush of cold air. He glanced up. Sure enough, the door was open.

He flew up the stairs, forcing his mind to believe Megan was there, somehow unhurt, waiting for him. He'd almost reached the top step when he heard her scream, a bloodcurdling yell that fractured his nerves and ripped away the last of his self-control.

The last time she'd screamed like that, he'd found her staring out over a broken railing, barely missing a plunge to her death.

MEGAN SCREAMED AGAIN as Mark pushed her head and upper body out over the railing. She grabbed hold of the railing, even lower than her bulging stomach, and stared at the sand below, swirling in the wind as if coaxing her down. A few inches more, and she'd lose her balance completely, but Mark was taunting her, a slow form of torture meant to drive her mad before he finished the job of killing her.

"Put your hands in the air and step away from Megan. Do it, *now*."

The brusque male voice topped the roar of the surf. Bart. He was here, or else she had dreamed him up to help her endure the nightmare. She twisted her body and tried to see behind Mark, but he pushed her head down so that all she could see was sand.

"Sorry, Copper, but I'm not backing away." Holding Megan with one arm, Mark pulled a gun from beneath his shirt with the other. "You want a war, you got it. Even if you shoot me, I'll have time to get a shot off and shove Megan over the railing. Either way, you both lose."

"I may lose, but you'll be dead," Bart warned, and she could tell by his voice he was stepping closer. "I won't miss from this range."

Only, Mark might not miss, either. Two dead men and her body slammed into the ground four stories below them. It was not the ending she had in mind. One arm was twisted behind her back. The other didn't have enough strength to do any real damage. But one second of advantage was all Bart would need.

She lowered her head and felt her body sway forward, gaining in momentum as it swept over the edge of the low railing, carrying her body with it. Then, reaching deep inside herself for all the strength she could muster, she swung her head back and rammed it against Mark.

The force of the contact crashed against her skull, knocking her senseless as the crack of gunfire from close range hammered inside her head. She didn't know who had fired, but she felt a hot stream of blood rolling down her arm as she collapsed to the floor at Mark's feet.

Chapter Eighteen

Megan opened her eyes and looked around. The room was dark except for the glow of sunset dancing among the shadows and gleaming against the white sheets. If this was heaven, it looked a lot like her bedroom at Pelican's Roost.

"Welcome back."

She stared at the voice, and turned to find Bart standing in the shadows, staring down at her. Sweet relief rolled through her. "You're alive."

"You're talking to an agent of the FBI. You surely didn't expect some sick jerk with a gun to best me." He sat down on the side of the bed and touched a hand to her cheek. "Of course, I didn't do it without a little help. You proved you have as hard a head as I do."

She touched her fingers to her temple, as it all came back. The head butting and the gunfire. "Who was shot?"

"Mark, but only in the gun hand. He's in jail now. The local police took him away. Along with the body of Roger Collier."

"Poor Roger."

"It was almost poor you as well."

"I remember. But I must have passed out."

"You fainted dead away. I had to tie up Mark with

some of the clothes in the cupola and carry you downstairs before I could even call the cops.'' He put the straw from a glass of water to her lips. ''Take a little sip. You sound hoarse.''

''That's because I perfected my screaming while I was trying to keep my balance.''

''I heard.''

''Saving me is getting to be a habit for you.''

''A habit I hope is ended. Loving you is the only habit I want to indulge in from here on out.''

''Loving me?''

He bent over and touched his lips to her forehead. ''Loving you, if you'll let me.''

''I made a couple of decisions while you were gone today, Bart. I'm not going to give the baby up for adoption.''

''What changed your mind?''

''My mother's diary, for one. I found it in one of the boxes in the cupola and read parts of it before Mark showed up on the scene. I know it was prying, but the secrets about who I am had gone on much too long.''

''Much too long, and they go much too deep.''

''I'm beginning to realize just how deep. But the diary isn't the only reason I want to keep the baby. You were right the other night. I love her already as much I love life itself. I want nothing more than to raise her. I was just too afraid of failure to give it a try. Only this time there'll be no secrets. When she's old enough, I'll tell her all about Jackie and Ben.''

''I'm very proud of you. I have some other news, though I'm not sure you'll like hearing it. I found out who your father is.''

''Lane Sellers.''

''How did you find out?''

"From Mark, though I don't know everything."

"Carlisle Sellers told me pretty much the whole story. He's very lucid for a man his age, especially one who's having as rough a time as he is just staying alive. It seems your mother and Jackie's father had an affair. He loved your mother, wanted to leave his wife and marry her, but Janelle Sellers realized she was pregnant with Jackie at the same time. She and Carlisle applied pressure and Lane decided to stay in the marriage."

"And no one ever told me the truth."

"That was because of a deal your mother made with Carlisle Sellers. He agreed to pay child support until you were eighteen, and to pay for your college education if your mother would keep his son's name out of this and never tell you that he was your father."

"So that's where the money came from all those years?"

"Apparently so. Janelle found out he was sending your mother checks and forbade him to ever set foot in her house again. Then a short while after her husband died, she told him that Jackie knew the truth and never wanted to speak to him again."

"That must have been at the same time she told Jackie he'd died."

"Apparently, Janelle Sellers never forgave her husband or your mother. But now that Carlisle Sellers is dying, he wants to see you and tell you that he's sorry he never made you part of his life. He's already put your name in his will, planned to split his rather sizable financial resources between you, Jackie and Mark. He hadn't heard about her death and I didn't tell him. I didn't think he could take the blow of that right now."

"So many secrets, so much deception for one little town. For one family." She took a hold of Bart's hand.

"At least I got to know Jackie, and I'll never be sorry for that. She always seemed like a sister to me. Now I find out she was my half sister."

"Which means the baby is actually kin to you."

"And now she'll share my life. But I don't think Mark even knew that the baby was Jackie's."

"No. From the little he said while we were waiting on the police to come and carry him away, I deducted as much. He was just going after you and Jackie. Killing the baby would have been lagniappe."

"But we didn't know that. Fate and a butcher called Joshua Caraway brought us together. If it hadn't been for him, you would have never come to Orange Beach and I'd likely be dead."

He stretched out beside her and trailed a finger down her cheek. "Fate is a very smart mistress, Megan. She must have known that when I met you, I'd fall in love with you."

"And I love you, Brad Cromwell or Dirk Cason or whoever you may be. Forever."

"Forever? You must still be delirious."

"Deliriously thankful that I'm alive and that I have you."

"Then I better buy some cigars. It looks like I'm about to become a dad."

"Don't you think you should become a husband first?"

"Absolutely. How about a Christmas wedding on the beach?"

"I think I can manage that, though I'm not sure what kind of wedding dress will fit."

"No matter what you wear, I'll think you're the most beautiful bride who ever said 'I do.'"

The baby kicked her approval as the handsome FBI agent took Megan in his arms. He kissed her. And she knew that forever with the man she loved would never be long enough.

Epilogue

December 25

"Clear the path. Pregnant bride coming through." The nurse rushed down the hospital corridor, pushing Megan wheelchair in front of her.

Dirk ran along side her, holding her hand as the latest contraction ripped through her lower body. The preacher was behind him, Bible in hand, waiting to finish the ceremony that the baby had interrupted.

The nurse wheeled her into the delivery room. "I guess the baby wanted in on the wedding."

"Why not?" Dirk answered. "She's been in on everything else."

"I can come back later," Reverend Forrester said. "We can easily do this once you're back home."

Megan breathed deeply and clutched her stomach. "No way. Just hurry and get to the I do's. I've come this far. I plan to finish it."

Dr. Brown popped through the door. "Looks like we're going to have a Christmas baby," he said, slipping his hand into a pair of sterile gloves. "Who needs a stork when Santa's flying?"

"A Christmas baby and a Christmas wedding," the nurse announced. "Megan was getting dressed for her wedding when she went into labor. The preacher followed them here."

"A wedding, is it? Then get on with it, but make it snappy." He winked and nodded to Forrester. "Babies follow their own schedule."

"I understand." Reverend Forrester pushed his wire-framed glasses up the bridge of his nose. "If it's okay with Dirk and Megan, I'll omit the usual rhetoric."

"It's fine by me," Dirk assured him.

"And with me," Megan added, between deep breaths.

"In that case, do you take Megan Lancaster to be your lawful wedded wife, to…?"

"I do," Dirk interrupted, as Megan's groans almost drowned out the preacher's voice.

"I do, too," she said, her voice cracking on the words. She grabbed Dirk's hands and squeezed as hard as she could."

"And that should do it," Dr. Brown said, getting in position to deliver the baby. "Now clear out, Reverend Forrester before I have you assisting."

Reverend Forrester backed away. "You two can sign the license later. I think you have your hands full right now."

"Breathe and push, Mrs. Dirk Cason," the doctor urged. "Breathe and push. This baby is on its way."

Mrs. Dirk Cason. A baby girl. The words spun in her head like cotton candy. Even in the pain, she knew she'd never had a sweeter moment in her life. "We're doing it, Jackie. We're doing it."

But the best reward came a seemingly endless time later when Doctor Brown finally placed the beautiful baby girl in her arms. Her heart swelled inside her. She touched her lips to the top of the baby's head. "I want to name her Jackie. Somehow, I have to believe that her mother is watching now, and that she knows her daughter is safe and loved."

Dirk trailed a finger down the baby's red cheek. "If Jackie is watching, then she has to be thankful she chose you to carry her child."

"And thankful that a very brave, handsome and persistent FBI agent came to our rescue."

"And here I am, a family man. And so happy I can hardly stand it." His mouth split into a wide grin and he patted his shirt pocket. "Care for a cigar?"

"No, all I want is you."

"Good, because you have me. Forever." He bent over the bed and kissed her lightly on the lips, but looked up as Reverend Forrester stuck his head back inside the door.

"I almost forgot. I now pronounce you man and wife. Merry Christmas, and you may kiss the bride."

Dirk did, while baby Jackie let them know that in all likelihood, it would not be a silent night.